Who is this beautiful little girl?

Her first smile captured Angus's heart forever. Small but perfect white teeth flashed in her dusty, tear-streaked face.

"What's your name?" he asked when she had eaten every scrap on the battered tin plate.

"J-yes." Her low voice had a tiny lisp.

Angus scratched his head. "J-yes?"

She nodded emphatically.

He mulled it over. "J-yes. Must be Joyous."

His keen gray eyes noted the way she responded. "Joyous. A good name."

"Where did you come from? How did you get here?"

Blank puzzlement crept into the poignant blue eyes that had laughed a moment earlier. She looked around her and fear returned to her face. "A long way. Men shouted. I...I hid in the dark. Someone carried me. I woke up here."

COLLEEN L. REECE is a prolific author with over sixty published books. With the popular *Storm Clouds over Chantel*, Reece established herself as a doyenne of Christian romance.

Books by Colleen L. Reece

HEARTSONG PRESENTS

HP1—A Torch for Trinity
HP2—Wildflower Harvest
HP7—Candleshine
HP8—Desert Rose
HP16—Silence in the Sage (with Gary Dale)
HP24—Whispers in the Wilderness (with Gary Dale)

ROMANCE READER—TWO BOOKS IN ONE

RR1—Honor Bound & The Calling of Elizabeth Courtland
RR4—To Love and Cherish & Storm Clouds over Chantel
RR6—Angel of the North & Legacy of Silver
RR8—A Girl Called Cricket & The Hills of Hope

Don't miss out on any of our super romances. Write to us at the following address for information on our newest releases and club information.

Heartsong Presents Reader's Service
P.O. Box 719
Uhrichsville, OH 44683

Veiled Joy

Colleen L. Reece

Heartsong Presents

ISBN 1-55748-427-9

COLLEEN L. REECE

PRINTED IN THE U.S.A.

prologue
1848

Sand swirled like a woman's veil, hiding all but a few blood red gleams from the dying sun. Angus McFarlane, desert rat that he was, shivered at the spectacle. "Jenny," he told his faithful prospecting companion, "we're in for it."

The faithful burro plodded steadily ahead, long ears drooping. The latest of many Jennies, she picked her way toward an unknown destination, always on the move, ever carrying picks and shovels, food, and a few cooking implements—and always water. She had watched a thousand sunrises, stumbled in the dark, crossed flooding rivers and desolate valleys. Time meant nothing. Only the presence of her master and a full stomach made life worthwhile. Now she bent her head against the rising wind and blindly followed the stocky, grizzled figure whose fingers tightened on her coarse mane.

For a single moment the sand lifted. "Praise be!" Angus increased his pace. The glimpse of stunted green ahead lent strength to his tired legs and sagging spirits. In the long years since he fled from a faithless sweetheart and an equally faithless friend to make the desert his home, Angus had learned the value of even the smallest living

5

tree and bush. He pushed on with the unerring instinct of a wolf on the trail, breathing heavily through the old scarf he had bound across his nose and mouth. It matched the one that protected Jenny, who quickened her slow steps.

"What is it, old girl?" Angus demanded when his burro brayed. "Water, I hope." He thought of the small amount left in his canteen—a sip for him, a cupped handful for Jenny.

Jenny brayed again and pulled a little to the left, becoming leader instead of follower now that the storm had made seeing impossible.

Angus clutched her mane and let her guide. Thank God for the knowledge He had put in critters when He created them. A dozen times they would have perished had it not been for the little burro's survival instincts. As he struggled in the heavy sand that sucked and grabbed at his feet, sometimes sinking into it, he was grateful for his companion and he remembered a legend of the desert.

According to the story, Jesus had appreciated so much that a little donkey had carried His mother on the way to Bethlehem and another had borne him in triumph into Jerusalem, that He wanted to reward them. The legend says that He placed a cross-shaped mark, lighter than the donkey's color, on the back of every burro. Some had a distinct mark, others had a faint and barely visible mark.

Just a story, yet Angus never stroked his beast of burden's cross-marked back without remembering Jesus. Although the prospector, whose keen eyes shone as gray as his hair, had lost faith in mankind, childhood teachings about God and His Son remained bright. Because of them, he held back from the vice and sin that led so many rough, lonely men downward. Never a day dawned without Angus's reading aloud from the *Auld Book*—his mother's Bible. And never did he sleep without a simple prayer of thankfulness that he and Jenny had been kept safely for another day.

The southwest trails that Angus's booted feet trod held invisible footprints of a man who stood far taller than his five-feet, eight-inch height. He traveled light and gave to those less fortunate. When Angus dreamed of striking it rich, thoughts of ragged children with hungry mouths filled those dreams. He had seen many such children, so, when a passing acquaintance told him gold had been discovered at Sutter's Mill in California, Angus turned Jenny north and west. God willing, he might pan enough gold and find enough small nuggets to send relief to God's children in need.

The sense, rather than sight, that Jenny had stopped, roused her master from his soliloquy. Sand stung his red-rimmed eyes but he dropped to his knees. The touch of water cooled his hands. He splashed it on his eyes, heard Jenny lapping noisily, then pulled his coat higher, turned his back to the storm, and waited.

With the coming of night, the wind lessened. The sand settled and no longer pelted the travelers. Bright stars poked holes in the heavens and a wary moon opened an eye to survey the waterhole. Angus munched a hard biscuit and ate sparingly of jerky, then drank the last of the water from the canteen. In the morning he would refill it from the opposite side of the small, shimmering pool away from where Jenny drank. Wrapped in a blanket, the man made old before his time murmured his prayer and slept.

He awakened to Jenny's bray. No longer did the burro's ears droop; both stood pricked up, listening.

Angus shook sand from his blanket and cocked his head. Only the sound of a small bird in a nearby bush reached him. "What's the matter, old girl?" He pulled one of her long ears. Jenny didn't move.

"Something strange here." Angus shifted position. The same sun that had slunk away, defeated by storm the night before, peeped over a distant rock outcropping then poured its warmth onto the land. Strange mounds of sand whipped into dunes rose around the waterhole. A slight sound drifted from behind the largest pile of sand.

Angus quietly slid his rifle from its resting place next to where he had slept and strode toward the dune, prepared in case a wild animal lay in wait. He rounded the pile of sand, stared. "What?" He shook his head and stared again.

The apparition was no mirage but a living, breathing child! Huddled with her arms across her chest, terror shone in her bright blue eyes. Reddish gold, disheveled curls framed a pale face and a dozen or so gilt freckles reflected the rising sun.

"Who are you? Where did you come from?" Angus

stepped nearer and she shrank back. He calculated her age as five or six, perhaps even seven. The child opened her mouth. No words came.

"Don't be afraid," he told her gruffly. "I'm just Angus. This is Jenny." The burro poked her nose over his shoulder to see what Angus had found.

Some of the fear left the little girl's face. She clutched her throat and tried to speak again but couldn't.

Angus turned on his heel, bumped the curious Jenny out of the way, and hurried back to the waterhole. He found where it fed into the small pool and filled his canteen. Moments later, he held it toward the child who eagerly reached for it with grimy hands. She drank and would have drunk more but Angus stopped her. "Take it easy, little one. There's plenty more. Are you hungry?"

She nodded and the sunshine danced in her sunset-colored hair. The prospector held out a weather-stained hand and she scrambled up and slid her fingers into his big palm. Something inside Angus melted at her trusting touch, the way she curled her small hand and trotted beside him. With deft skill he shaved jerky into a little water and softened it. He toasted the last of the hard biscuits and brought her breakfast. "Sorry it isn't more," he apologized.

Her first smile captured Angus's heart forever. Small but perfect white teeth flashed in her dusty, tear-streaked face.

"What's your name?" he asked when she had eaten

every scrap on the battered tin plate.

"J-yes." Her low voice had a tiny lisp.

Angus scratched his head. "J-yes?"

She nodded emphatically.

He mulled it over. "J-yes. Must be Joyous."

His keen gray eyes noted the way she responded. "Joyous. A good name."

"Where did you come from? How did you get here?"

Blank puzzlement crept into the poignant blue eyes that had laughed a moment earlier. She looked around her and fear returned to her face. "A long way. Men shouted. I-I hid in the dark. Someone carried me. I woke up here." She wrinkled her nose and looked at her slender hands. "Dirty."

Angus produced a battered pan with heated water and dug a tiny piece of soap out of the saddlebags. "I'll just mosey around for a while. You get washed." He awkwardly took out a shirt big enough to wrap around her a dozen times. "Put that on and I'll wash your clothes." He looked dubiously at her stockings and small shoes, totally unsuitable for the wilderness, then pulled out a clean but mended pair of his socks. "Wear these. The sun will dry your clothes fast." He started away then stopped, held by the fear in her eyes. "I won't go far. See, Jenny's here to keep you company." The fear subsided and Angus walked away warmed by her smile.

"Where did she come from, Lord?" He often talked to God while he traveled. Many times he felt God near and cherished the feeling. It kept him from loneliness even when he was alone except for the burro.

Now he doffed his old hat and shook his head. "Worse, what am I going to do with her? First thing's to see if I can find her folks, I reckon."

Yet a thorough scouring of the north, west, and south over the next few days failed to unearth a single clue to the mysterious coming of the girl. Angus came to believe something had happened to her so shocking that she simply couldn't remember any more than she'd told him. After a few futile attempts at questioning, he gave it up. With the adaptability of children, she quickly fell into his way of life. Except for once or twice when she cried out in the night and he comforted her, Joyous acted perfectly happy and wove herself into the fabric of the prospector's heart.

A week passed and Angus knew the time had come to move on. Yet he still must search east of the little waterhole. As usual, he left Jenny with Joyous. "Don't be worried if I'm gone for a while," he said. "There's fried rabbit and sourdough biscuits for when you get hungry."

She didn't argue but the look on her face stopped him cold. It would take far longer today than when he'd gone before.

"Reckon you'd better go with me, Joy." His big arms opened and she flew into them. Fifteen minutes later, she bobbed up and down on Jenny's back, chattering about every bird or ground squirrel or tiny flower she saw.

The final search bore fruit. A half-mile east of the waterhole, Angus, Joy, and Jenny found a man sprawled under the scant shade of a mesquite, desert garb tattered and torn. Wasted by evident hunger and hardship, his breath came slow and uneven.

"Do you know him?" Angus asked the little girl.

She looked at the man. "He carried me."

Angus's heart leaped. "From where?"

"I don't know." The curtain between memory and reality had fallen again.

Despite everything Angus could do, the stranger died the next day without disclosing the secret of Joy and how she had come into his possession. Angus tried a last time to rouse her remembrance. "Was he your father? Your daddy?"

A spark flashed into her blue, blue eyes. "No." She dug her fists into hips and emphatically shook her head before a flood of tears came.

Angus said no more. He buried the stranger in a shallow grave and formed a cairn from nearby stones to protect the body from marauding animals. Perhaps someday it would be necessary to return to this spot. In the meantime. . . .

"Joy." Angus felt a lump form in his throat. "Would you like to call me Daddy?" He quickly added, "I'll do everything I can to find your folks but 'til then, we're pardners."

She climbed into his lap. "Daddy Angus." Her small hand twined itself in his grizzled hair. "Pardners."

"We can't do anything else here," he told her. A great determination grew within him. "Before I...we got caught in the sandstorm—which, by the way, I'll never figure out just how you got to the waterhole from where we found that fellow—anyway, Jenny, here, and I were on our way to find gold. How'd you like for me to have enough money to buy you pretty things?"

She smiled her enchanting smile and fingered the torn lace on her dress. Every few days he made her bathe while he washed the dress for her. "I need a new dress."

"You sure do." He eyed the torn garment with distaste. "Let's see what we can do. I'm no dressmaker but I bet we can fix you up all right." He carefully observed the general cut of her simple white dress, the lace-trimmed dress that had baffled him. How could a child in the desert possess such a thing? Even to his inexperienced eyes it looked like the fine dresses his cousins used to wear back home in the East.

Angus fashioned a gown from an old blanket worn soft by use that wouldn't scratch Joy. He cut holes with his hunting knife, stitched with the big old needle and coarse thread he always carried, and even braided a belt from narrow strips of the same blanket. "Not the world's best but it will do until we get somewhere to but you some clothes," he grunted.

Charmed with the freedom of the wide skirt he had made to give her room to run and ride, Joy hooked one foot behind her other ankle and curtsied. "Thank you, Daddy."

She carefully folded up the little white dress and handed it to Angus when he warned, "We must always keep this. Someday it may help us find your real family."

"You're my daddy. I don't want a real family!" With a flash of the rare temper he'd seen only a time or two, Joy flung herself headlong into his arms.

Angus swallowed hard. What had a desert rat to do with a child who obviously had been raised in a genteel, perhaps luxurious home? He gently laid one hand on the curls he smoothed for her night and morning and offered a silent prayer. *God, thank You that I was here when she needed me. You know I've done my best to make things right. Now, it's up to You.* But he inwardly shuddered at the thought of a possible future without Joy, should God lead them to those among whom she belonged.

By the time Angus, slowed by a child who was sturdy yet tired sooner than he, arrived in California and got to Sutter's Mill, the majority of good claims had been staked by the thousands who had poured in after the initial finding of gold nuggets.

James Marshall, a carpenter, had been hired by John Sutter, a pioneer trader, to help build a sawmill on the American River. Sutter had received a land grant in 1839 to a large portion of land in the Sacramento Valley. Marshall discovered the first nuggets in 1848 just before the signing of the Treaty of Guadalupe Hidalgo, which ended the Mexican War and ceded southwestern lands to the United States

From desert solitude to gold rush fury, Angus and Joy plunged. If those seeking their fortune hadn't been so engrossed in their own pursuits, a grizzled prospector and a striking child such as Joy could never have escaped gossip. Angus used his canny Scottish upbringing to survey the situation and act accordingly. Instead of rushing to claim or grab land alongside others, he quietly and wisely took Joy and Jenny upstream and away from the hordes who resembled nothing more than bees in a hive in the frenzy. Joy soon learned that a *cradle* separated gold from worthless stone by rocking gravel and water until the lighter materials sifted out and left the gold. Her scream of excitement when flakes the color of her hair and occasional small nuggets appeared, brought a smile to Angus's austere face.

"We don't care about having all the gold the Almighty put in California," he explained to her. "What we need is enough to take care of you."

"You and Jenny, too," she insisted. The blanket dress had given way to calico; the golden curls were neatly woven into braids.

"Of course." Yet Angus's heart lurched. It simply wasn't believable that their roads would always be together. Someday, Joy might well be taken from him.

In the months that followed, the thousands who poured in seeking gold came to pose a threat in Augus' mind. Neither did he like having Joy growing up in these surroundings. He said nothing to her of his plans but, after he discovered an extremely rich pocket and cleaned it of nuggets and dust that left them well-off, though not wealthy, he took the child on his knee.

"Joy, I've been thinking. Aren't you getting tired of all the noise and crowds and digging for gold? How would you like to leave here?"

She solemnly peered at him with her incredibly blue eyes surrounded with golden lashes the same shade as her braids. "Would you, Daddy? Would Jenny go?"

"Yes, child." His arms tightened around her.

"Where will we go?" She snuggled close.

A thousand times he had asked himself the same question. The desert he loved offered little to a child. No chance for an education, beyond what he could teach her.

She already reads far beyond her years, a little voice inside tempted. *From the Bible, too. She's learned to write and to spell and to do numbers the same way. What better teaching can she have?*

"Is there somewhere you'd like to go?" he asked.

Joy thought for a long time. Then she sat upright and said, "Somewhere faraway where it is quiet. I want to see the stars, and hear birds sing instead of people yelling." The same fear she had shown so long before, when she told him she remembered men yelling, crept into her face.

"We'll go, Joy. Tomorrow," Angus promised.

The next day the inseparable trio left the gold rush area to find the faraway place Joyous McFarlane, as she called herself, longed for. They didn't look back.

one

The sailing ship, *Promised Land*, rose and fell with the tossing waves, waiting for the human cargo she would take to America. A swarm of humanity, bent beneath the possessions they could carry, filed aboard amidst shouts from the sailors, children's cries, and a keening, growing wind.

Seventeen-year-old Britton O'Donnell's arms tightened about his baby sister, Katie, and whispered, "Don't cry, *mavourneen*.* Mother and Father and the lads are just behind." His Gaelic pronunciation softened the words; they sounded like *mither* and *feyther*.

Katie snuggled closer and hid her face in his rough, hand-made sweater. Brit's dark head bent above her. How would such a mite fare on the long journey? He lifted his gaze to the scowling sky. His Irish blue eyes with their thick black lashes took on a gray cast. "Irish eyes set in with a sooty finger" tradition described them well.

"Coffin boats, that's what they are," someone next to them spat. "They pack us in like animals, furnish bad food for our good money. Only by the grace of God will any of us be alive even if the vessel isn't lost at sea."

Brit whipped around, angry color filling his smooth

face. "Then why are you going, man?"

The speaker stared at him and said sourly, "Are you an Irishman asking such a question?"

Brit's wide shoulders sagged. His six-foot frame trembled. This wasn't the first time he'd heard the words coffin boats. Reports from those who had immigrated before came back. Everything the sallow-faced man had said was true. Ships such as the *Promised Land* pledged hope but too often ended in death, especially for the sick and weak.

Suddenly Brit wished he could flee from the peril ahead. He glanced despairingly at his parents and the two little brothers whose wide-eyed gazes showed understanding beyond what children should have. *God, help us,* he silently prayed. He looked at his once-strong father, his patient and loving mother, and wanted to cry out, "Why are we here? Wouldn't we be better to have stayed in County Cork?"

The words behind his lips died aborning. Whatever lay before them couldn't be worse than their remaining in Ireland in 1850. The O'Donnell family, along with hundreds of thousands of others, had been brought to their knees by the terrible potato famine. Unlike the 750,000 who perished between 1845 and 1847 while the potatoes rotted in the ground, the O'Donnells had hung on somehow. Through starvation and disease, the agony of Ireland's cry, *Tha shein uchrais,* which means "I am hungry," faith in God and grim determination kept the wolf a few feet from the O'Donnells' door. Neighbors not so fortunate huddled in dark cabins, wore rags, and starved to death in smoke-filled rooms. The old folks in cities begged in whispers, crowded in tenements. Many Irish poor could not pay rent and were evicted. Cities burned to rubble. Dead lay in the streets.

Brit thought of the rich landowners who lived elsewhere and familiar rage rose within him. Instead of helping their tenants by raising other food crops for the poor, they turned to cattle, hogs, and grain, shipping them to England from the major Irish ports at great profit—while the poor continued to die.

Although the government halfheartedly worked to stem the tide by establishing workhouses that offered scant shelter and food, Brit had heard again and again that those who ran them labeled poverty as a "disease" rather than a product of the times. The O'Donnells vowed to die together rather than claim a place in a workhouse and be separated, subject to all manner of disease and to have body and soul held together through small servings of porridge or thin soup.

Brit blinked involuntary tears, thickened by the drizzle of rain that had begun. He noted the new silver in his mother's hair beneath the crocheted cap. In spite of his anger and dread, his heart warmed within him, remembering the day Father burst into their thatched cottage with news.

"The Ursuline nuns at the Blackrock convent have received ninety pounds for a single piece of crochet made by the poor children of the lacemaking school," he told them.

"Ninety pounds!" Never had Brit dreamed of such an amount. His eyes gleamed. "Father, we must learn to crochet."

"Aye. 'Twill be the saving of Ireland. Thanks be to God."

In the days and weeks that followed, even the little boys' fingers grew proficient at making lace. Every bit of money not needed to keep the family fed was carefully hoarded. For, as Father said, "We have no hope here. We must save and sail for America. 'Tis a new land with new hope." Tears sometimes glistened in his eyes and Brit knew how hard the rending apart from the rolling green hills and sparkling rivers would be for them all. Yet, deep in his heart, the yearning to be free from the misery that kept Ireland under a black cloud grew until 1850 when passage money had been secured for the O'Donnells.

"Father was right," Brit murmured to himself and shifted Katie a little higher before closing the gap between himself and the person just ahead of him in line. "Crocheting made the difference to the O'Donnells and thousands of others." He thought of how the world clamored for Irish lace. So many different kinds, so many names. *Nun's Lace. Poor man's lace. Shepherd's knitting,* that heavier crochet work that formed caps and sweaters from wool strands home-spun from sheep, even from strands caught in bushes. Commissions from export firms kept fingers flying between farm chores—outdoors to utilize the last ray of sunlight, on hillsides, by peat fires—and Irish crochet lace became regarded as a harvest.

"Da." The smallest boy who hung from Mr. O'Donnell's hand tugged. "I want to go home. I don't like it here."

The other lad chimed in and clutched his fathers coat tails. "We'll work hard and make more lace."

If Brit lived to be a hundred he would never forget the pain in his father's eyes when the tall man so like his oldest son quietly said, "Home is when we're together. Come now, lads, it's our turn to board."

On reluctant feet, the O'Donnells passively stepped onto the ill-named *Promised Land*, but Brit's rebellious heart held no passiveness. Before being herded with the others down into an abyss far from the fresh air and comfort of the wealthy, he set his lips in a straight line. The O'Donnells would endure whatever it took to be free from their poverty stricken native land. But, when they reached America, things would be different.

Surrounded by moans and tears, fetid air, and the stench of too many people in too small a space, Brit O'Donnell vowed, *God, I will never let my family have to go through anything like this again. I will accept any honorable work, no matter how mean or low, so long as it will not offend Thee. One day Father, Mother, Katie, and the lads will know comfort again. Protect us by Thy might on this terrible trip. Help us to care for those less fortunate for the sake of Thy Son, Amen.*

Brit soon lost track of the weak ones who sickened and died. The man who had braved the dangers in spite of his own prophecy about unbearable conditions lasted only a week. Others followed. The food given them became coarser and less nourishing—soup, thinner than the heaving seas the *Promised Land* sailed, with bits of meat the O'Donnells didn't dare identify, brackish water, and precious little of that.

"How can anyone treat others so?" Brit cried out in desperation when, during a raging storm, the miserable occupants of the ship's hold were securely locked in. "If the ship goes down we have no hope of survival." He pounded on the door at the top of the companionway* and kicked it with heavy shoes.

"The captain knows well the rabble, as he calls us, is ready to mutiny," a fiery eyed man muttered.

A thrill of horror went through Brit. He had heard of crews and passengers who took a ship into their own hands although the punishment for mutineers was death. Yet for a time his tired, troubled heart wondered if anything could be worse than the conditions surrounding him. So far he and his family had managed to escape the ever-present sickness, the threat of being robbed in their sleep. How long could they endure? Fellow travelers, if such a wretched mass could be called so, scorned the O'Donnells' quiet nightly prayers. They had been cursed and spat at by those who openly declared that if a God existed, He had forsaken them.

*wooden staircase

Did Brit's mother suspect his thoughts as she had so many times in their quiet country life that felt like eons before? She leaned close and whispered for his ears alone from Chapter Ten of Matthew, " 'And ye shall be hated of all men for my name's sake; but he that endureth to the end shall be saved.' "

Brit drew in a deep breath of the foul air, choked, and clung to the verse. The storm grew more violent. The *Promised Land* shrieked and groaned in harmony with its pitiful occupants until with every plunge Brit knew the death angel sat on the mast waiting. Flickering light from wicks dipped in grease showed naked fear in the faces around him.

"Come close," Mr. O'Donnell ordered. "Remember, whatever happens, we're together. We will live in the Lord or die in the Lord, but it will be together."

Home is when we're together. Brit took Katie in his lap, bowed his head, and waited. Nausea hit him and he thrust her away none too soon. Around them the sounds and smell of others vomiting increased the awfulness.

Sometime later, the ship's motion lessened to a gentle roll. Brit opened his eyes, amazed that he'd slept. He looked from face to face of the scores of those who had weathered this last storm. Something tore free inside of him. He would stand it no longer.

He leaped to his feet and up the companionway. "Listen to me!"

His clear, ringing voice dragged weary, apathetic eyes

open. A few strong men, including the one who had spoken
of mutiny, sat up and stared. A low mumble of protest
against anyone who ordered them to do anything began.

Brit cut it short. "We paid our passage money in good
faith. We've been herded and starved and treated like
animals. If the ship had gone down last night, we'd have
been trapped. We must never let it happen again!"

A feeble cheer rose. A man stood and climbed to the step
beneath Brit. Then another and another. "What can we
do?" someone cried.

"This." Brit turned and assaulted the door but the sturdy
outside bar held firm. "Let us out," he bellowed.

A hundred throats took up the cry. Louder and louder
the din grew until the heavy footsteps outside the barricad-
ed door were barely audible.

"Stand back," came a roar from the other side of the
heavy door.

Brit and his comrades backed down the companionway
and stood waiting.

The scrape of wood against wood then the creak of the
door to the deck opening preceded the entrance of a
Goliath and a dozen sailors, who catapulted down the
companionway until they faced Brit. "What's going on
down here?"

"You will not be for barring us in again." Brit's deadly
voice and Irish blue eyes that changed to slate gray with
emotion stopped the giant.

"Who says?"

"I do." Brit didn't move, even when the fellow's foul breath hit him full in the face."

"And I."

"And I." A wall of driven men edged forward.

The jailer stepped back but howled, "What will you do, you Irish scum?" The flicker of fear in the beefy face and ox eyes encouraged Brit, even when the man added, "You've caused enough trouble with your shrieking and disturbing the other passengers."

His unfortunate choice of words completed the transformation of those he ruled from debilitated men to an army seeking justice.

"Kill him!" someone screamed. "Kill them all, the rotten landowners who threw us from our homes and let our children starve!"

Aghast, Brit stared. Never in his wildest anger had he planned anything like this. "Stop!" He seized control of the rapidly growing violence. "Will we be no better than those who persecute us?"

His sheer daring won him a little time. His mind invented and rejected a dozen solutions.

"Feed us proper, keep the door unlocked or we'll fire the ship," a man called from behind Brit.

The jailer's face turned to parchment but he gathered his contempt and sneered, "Liar. You'd be the first to burn."

Brit noticed a slight tremble in the man's lips even while he spoke. Could they bluff him? *God, help.*

A dozen others staunchly agreed they would set the

Promised Land on fire rather than be submitted to what they had gone through the previous night.

"You, boy. Would you willingly see your family burn?"

The wisdom of Solomon fell on Brit. Instead of answering yea or nay he lowered his voice until those behind him had to strain to catch his answer. "Is it any worse to burn than to die trapped in a sinking ship?"

The jailer's jaw dropped. He backed away, into a group of sailors behind him. "Get the captain," he barked, then froze in position.

The captain arrived panting and furious. "Are you mad?" he hissed into Brit's face, who still held the lead position. "Mutiny is punishable by death!"

Brit felt a restraining spirit that warned him to weigh each word. "Sir, no one has threatened mutiny—so far."

A rumble of approval behind him brought even more rage into the captain's heavily featured face. "Then, what's this all about?"

"They say they'll burn the ship, sir," the jailer spit out.

"You are mad. Clap this man in irons," the captain ordered.

Before the sailors behind him could move, several of the largest Irishmen jerked Brit back and stood in front of him, arms crossed, a living barricade. "You'll not be taking the lad. He made no threat—I did. All O'Donnell did was ask if 'twas any worse to burn than to die trapped and locked in should the ship go down."

"I can put you all in the brig," the captain fumed. Yet,

when he observed the way the fighting Irish had rallied behind their leaders, his lips set in an upside-down tilt. Even the children and all who weren't too sick to rise stood accusing him with their eyes. Gone were prejudices and differences of opinion, lost in the common cause: the need to survive.

"What do you want?" the captain finally asked.

Brit thrust through to the forefront. "Decent food—and don't say you haven't any. We know how your other passengers eat. More water. Medicine for our sick. . .a doctor if there's one aboard. And your word as captain of this ship that before God Almighty there will be no more locking of us in this pesthole."

For a moment he thought he'd gone too far. Blue hate filled the captain's eyes. Brit's fingers curled into fists and his nails cut into the palms of his hands.

Even in defeat the captain clutched at his dignity. "I make no promises about. . .the medicine." He started away then turned on his heel. "Jailer, see about food and water. And don't—" he broke off. "O'Donnell, is it?"

Brit nodded.

"Do I have your word before God Almighty there will be no taking advantage, no roaming of the *Promised Land* and stealing should the locks be unturned?"

"You have."

"So be it. Jailer, there is no need to lock them up for the remainder of the journey." He gathered the remnants of his authority and marched up the companionway, ramrod stiff in spite of a delayed cheer.

"Weren't you 'fraid?" Brit's little brother asked when he worked his way back to the family.

"I guess I was too angry to be afraid." Brit tousled the lad's hair. "Besides, I felt God's spirit inside me."

"Did God tell you what to say?" the little boy persisted.

"I believe He did. I couldn't lie and He's promised to direct us in danger if we turn to Him."

True to his word, the captain saw to it that more palatable food reached his poorest passengers—and extra water.

A sour- looking doctor who obviously considered himself above tending "Irish scum" came a few times for a cursory examination of those in steerage and doled out inadequate amounts of medicine to a few. "No sense wasting it on those who are almost gone," he callously pronounced.

Part of Brit wanted to shake the charlatan until he rattled but a selfish part rejoiced that Katie received the drops to help her get well. He thanked God the rest of the family hadn't been stricken and prayed for those who had.

Then one glorious day the long-awaited call sounded like Gabriel's trumpet, thrilling the souls of all on board the *Promised Land.* "Land, ho!"

"Gather your bundles," Mrs. O'Donnell told her family. "Britton, you take Katie, please."

The listless child brightened when they made their way into sunlight so strong those pitiful immigrants who had been so long in the bowels of the *Promised Land* blinked and stood dazed.

"Move along, there," came the order, but Brit paused by the ship's rail and stared ahead. Somewhere in America lay rolling green hills that resembled those in Ireland. Somewhere rivers and streams ran clear and laughed their way to the sea. Somewhere in this new land he would find a home for his family.

He looked at his father, worn and spent with worry and lack of good food and water and air. His mother, who never let her family end the day without giving thanks. His brothers, frankly round-eyed at the sight of buildings, a bustling harbor, that loomed ahead.

Then Brit held Katie up so she could see over the heads of others transfixed by the knowledge they had actually arrived. "Look, *mavourneen*. We are together and this will be our new home."

He shifted her to his shoulder, reached for a worn satchel with his free hand, and followed the long, uneven line of survivors until he set foot on a land of freedom and promise. Hope in his heart, a prayer of praise on his lips to the God Who had sustained them, Brit O'Donnell faced his future.

And he didn't look back.

two

Seven years after the O'Donnells stumbled off the miserable ship *Promised Land* into the United States of America, twenty-three-year old Brit stepped into the cool spring air of April 1857.

What strange paths they had traveled! First, the tenements of New York City along with so many others from their homeland, huddled together for protection against a new and sometimes unfriendly land.

From the very start, Brit's strength served him well. He landed a job as a stevedore on the docks, grimly ignored those who called him a black Irish mick, and did his work so well even the meanest hecklers developed a healthy respect for him—and for the fists he used only in the most dire of circumstances. He had prayed about fighting and at last realized that until he proved himself he would never be free.

It took just two quick battles to establish his prowess—the first a thorough drubbing of the biggest bully on the dock; the second, more of the same to the bully's best friend. Ironically, those two did a complete about-face and became Brit's guardians! Never could he have found two more loyal protectors, once their blackened eyes reopened.

A chance encounter with a shipowner led to a night watchman job in addition to his long hours of cargo handling. His mother protested but Brit reminded, "Our Father can be with me just as well there as anywhere." Mr. O'Donnell agreed. With decent food and rest, he had regained much of his splendid strength.

The whole family's dream was to save enough to find and purchase farming land. Sprawling cities grated on those used to the peace and quiet of pastoral scenes. The screech of crowds contrasted sharply with roosters crowing, hens clucking and the garbage-filled, narrow streets prevented even taking in great breaths of air.

Months slipped into years, Katie and the lads grew, and one day enough money hid in the old sugar bowl for the great exodus.

"Maine," the O'Donnells decided in family consultation. "It has coasts and rivers and trees. We can feel at home there. Other Irish families have migrated to Maine."

Brit added, "Aroostook Country in the eastern upland region has fertile soil. We can grow potatoes again."

"And continue to make lace," Mrs. O'Donnell added. Some of the sugar bowl money had come from the exquisite lace she crocheted, adding flowers and symbols of America to the shamrocks and rosettes of the traditional Irish crochet lace.

Faith in God and hard work resulted in the establishment

of the family on the farm they had dreamed of for so long. Not only potatoes but milk and butter and eggs would help keep the family prosperous.

Brit pitched in as wholeheartedly as the rest yet his eyes often looked westward. Tales of riches and opportunity stirred something within him. Now, on this misty morning that reminded him of County Cork just before the sun rose, he lifted his face to the sky. "Lord, I have kept my promise. I have worked hard and always at jobs that would not dishonor Thee. Is this restlessness Thy way of preparing me for something new?" His low voice sounded loud in the clear air. Before him lay fields cultivated and planted with his own hands. Behind him lay neatly kept home and outbuildings.

Gaze steady on the glimpse of sea in the distance from which the sun would burst into glory, Brit continued, "The lads are old enough now to work with Father. Katie, young as she is, already knows cookery enough to run our home should Mother fall ill." He laughed at the thought. God had restored health to the family. Brit's heart swelled. "Is my longing of Thee?"

A streak of pink, a glow of rose, and the never-ending wonder of the sun's climbing into the sky and reflecting in the sea stilled further prayer. Humbled as always by the beauty of his Heavenly Father's creation, Brit waited until the pink and rose faded into a warm yellow glow then turned toward the barn and morning chores.

Not until the family had finished their morning meal and

Katie and the lads had vanished on pursuits of their own for the hour allowed before chores did Mrs. O'Donnell, with her uncanny knowledge of her son's feelings and thoughts, placidly say, "Son, you're a man now. Twenty-four you'll be in another month. Your father and I can never thank you enough for all these years you've worked and sweated and never once complained."

He started to reply but she raised her hand and continued, "Your father and I feel it's time you be making your own life." She offered him more Irish soda bread, lumpy and warm, then passed preserves from blackberries the family had picked the summer before. "If it's in your heart to leave us, we understand." In the emotion-charged moment, her face settled into its usual laugh-crinkled expression. "It's not as if you've set your heart on a pretty colleen and long for a farm and wee ones."

"I haven't had time." Brit grinned to cover the depth of love and the feeling of being set free when he hadn't even realized he'd been caged.

His father's gaze, blue-gray as his son's, rested on Brit. "Mind when you find her she's like your mother."

"As if I wouldn't." Britt grew serious. "Just this morning I talked with God about the future."

"We've seen it coming. Rightly so," his mother said fiercely. "Is it west you'll be going?"

"Why, how did you know?" Brit couldn't hide his astonishment.

"There's a look that's crept into your eyes when you

turned toward the setting sun," she gently replied. "Go
with God."

A fortnight later, Brit O'Donnell began his long journey
west, too late for the California Gold Rush, but intrigued
at the idea of being a pioneer and seeing unknown places.
When his father offered to buy passage for him to California on shipboard, he shuddered and refused. "I'll go by
land. The trip on the *Promised Land* killed any wish for
ocean voyages! And I'll not hurry. I'm strong and can
work hard." His eyes twinkled. "If I find wealth in
California, will you come?" He caught the quick exchange of glances, the shadow of parting, and hastily said,
"Why don't we talk such things when the gold's in my
pocket!"

The same versatility that had helped in the past rose to
aid Brit on his westward trek. He worked his way instead
of touching the little hoard carefully sewn into his jacket
lining by his mother's nimble fingers. Personable, un-
afraid of the meanest tasks, good-natured, he slowly
moved west, driving teams for those who fell ill on the
wagon train he joined at Independence, helping at roundups on ranches where he tarried, repairing broken wheels
and machinery. He spent the winter months trapping in the
Rocky Mountains and added to his assets. In the spring he
pushed on, got caught in a late blizzard in the Sierra
Nevadas, and, but for the grace of God, would have
perished.

Lured by his long absence from the sea, Brit rode into Monterey early in the fall of 1858, unkempt but unbowed. He filled his lungs with good salt air and curiously examined the strange, Spanish-looking homes so different from Irish and New England architecture. Quickly reviewing what little he knew of the city, he remembered Monterey had been under Spanish, Mexican, and then American rule, and had been California's capital city until 1850. He liked the palm trees with their downbent fronds and the lacy ironwork fences and gates behind which aristocratic Spanish and Mexican high-caste families dwelled.

One of the gates stood open. A long winding road vanished into a stand of oak trees and tall bushes covered with brilliant flowers. Brit slowed Shamrock, the bay horse he had purchased and renamed when he left the Rockies in the spring. He stared open-mouthed at the delicacy of the patterns in the gate. "It looks like our lace," he told Shamrock.

Before the gelding could do more than lazily turn his head, the rapid pound of hoofbeats jerked Brit's attention away from the gate and to the road inside. Gravel spurted when a magnificent white horse rounded the clump of oaks and headed toward him at a dead run. Why didn't the rider rein him in? Then, Brit saw the slipping saddle that could not have been cinched properly and the terrified face of a white-faced boy no older than the lads at home. Chalk white against midnight black hair, the boy fought valiantly to remain in the saddle.

"He'll never do it," Brit muttered and turned Shamrock so they'd be parallel when the runaway exploded through the gate.

The white stallion stretched out, ready for a long run. The saddle slipped more.

"Kick your feet out of the stirrups!" Brit shouted.

The rider obeyed and tried to rein the stallion in.

Tense, Brit waited helplessly, praying the boy could stay on just a few feet farther. If he fell now, he'd be impaled on the pointed iron fence.

With a mighty leap, the stallion swept through the gate. The saddle turned down toward the horse's belly. The rider tried to rein in his mount but could not.

"Now, Shamrock!" Brit spurred his bay, the first time ever. With a start of surprise, the fine animal sprang alongside the stallion. Brit pressed his knees into his horse's sides and gripped like glue. His right arm shot out, caught the endangered boy by the back of his shirt, and yanked. The shirt tore, but not before Brit had its owner face down across Shamrock while the white stallion thundered away riderless.

"Whoa, boy!" Brit pulled hard on the reins and curbed Shamrock's headlong rush after the low white streak. The bay snorted and reluctantly slowed, then stopped.

Brit slid from the saddle and dropped the reins. Shamrock had been taught to stand once this happened. "Are you hurt?" He assisted the struggling boy upright and onto the ground.

"No, señor. Just very angry."

Brit could believe it. The boy's midnight eyes held rage at the ignominious defeat at the hands of the stallion.

"Gracias." The slim rider shook his head in the direction the stallion had taken and proudly drew himself up. "Sol always tries to throw me but he never can." His thin nostrils dilated. "It was the saddle. A new peon in the stable and...." He shrugged and lifted one arched eyebrow indicating that surely señor understood.

Brit squelched the desire to laugh at the haughty manner. Instead he said solemnly, "Shall I go round up Sol?"

"Si. Papa will be furious, enraged, distraught should harm come to Sol. I will wait here." He gracefully leaned against the still-open iron gate. "When you return and drive this bad horse inside, I will slam the gate shut and he will be caught."

The minute he got out of earshot, Brit chuckled. His first encounter with Castilian aristocracy had its amusing moments. He urged Shamrock into a run, wondering where the rescue might lead. If he'd expected excitement, he was doomed to disappointment.

Once free of his rider, the white stallion fell to the lure of rich grass not more than a half-mile form the hacienda. He raised his head and neighed, turned and showed Shamrock his heels.

It didn't intimidate the range-trained bay gelding, yet Brit respected the wicked glint in the stallion's eyes and knew driving Sol back would be impossible. The months he'd spent on roundups served well when his lean fingers reached for his lariat. The rope sang and a wide noose dropped over Sol's shoulders and tightened. Before the stallion could protest the indignity, Shamrock braced all four feet while Brit jumped from the saddle and raced to the protesting horse. In moments, he had jerked the saddle into place and had whacked Sol so he couldn't blow himself up and end up with another round of saddle slipping. Brit slipped his left boot into the stirrup and swung aboard, with Shamrock still holding steady. He tightened the reins and pulled Sol's head high. If the white stallion got his head down between his knees, there would be bucking.

With the unpredictability of his kind, Sol turned docile, obviously used to a struggle then giving in when mastered. Brit beckoned Shamrock, recoiled his lariat, and turned Sol toward the hacienda with the bay just far enough behind to avoid any wicked kicking the stallion might decide to do.

"Señor!" The boy leaped from his indolent pose when the little caravan came near. Perfect teeth shone white in his olive-skinned face that had returned to its natural color.

Brit rubbed his eyes with one hand. He had left one slim youth; now two awaited him, identically garbed in dark riding clothes lavishly trimmed with silver and braid. The second figure only reached the boy's shoulder, but the same black velvet eyes watched the trio's approach and a hint of softly curling dark hair peeped from beneath the black hat with its silver filigree band.

"Younger brother," Brit surmised. "Probably as proud as the peacock I saved from a nasty spill." He rode into what he now saw was a large courtyard and followed the direction of the boy's pointing finger toward large, well-tended stables a good quarter of a mile from the long, low hacienda itself.

The two dark figures raced up soon after Brit dismounted and tossed Sol's reins to an apprehensive, waiting peon whose swarthy skin showed his rank as clearly as his occupation.

A volley of sibilant Spanish from the smaller figure caused the peon to yank his enormous hat off, cast despairing eyes toward the sky, and wordlessly spread his hands in supplication for mercy. The liquid voice didn't cease until Brit cut in.

"Don't be too hard on him. It happens to us all. Horses are smart. They know if they swell up, the saddle won't be cinched up tight enough."

"Señor is right, Dolores," the older boy said.

"Dolores!" Brit stared at the smaller figure.

"But of course." The boy's eyes opened wide. "I am Carlos Montoya and this is my sister, Dolores."

"I beg your pardon, miss, uh. . .señorita," Brit stammered.

A laugh that tinkled and trickled like a happy waterfall accompanied the cascade of dark curls that fell when she snatched off her sombrero. No man hearing that laugh could mistake Dolores Montoya's identity. Brit couldn't take his gaze off her. In spite of the boyish garb, her femininity shone through. She couldn't be more than an inch over five feet and her beautifully proportioned body topped by a proud head spoke the word patrician with every movement. Brit had seen attractive, yes, even beautiful Irish colleens. He had never seen any girl or woman who surpassed this Spanish señorita.

"Señor, what is it you are called?" Her voice matched her entire bearing in exquisiteness.

"Brit. Britton O'Donnell." He awkwardly doffed his cap.

A puzzled frown marred the beauty of the white forehead. "You are. . .Yankee?"

He noted the disdain and shook his head. "No. I am an Irishman." His head unconsciously lifted with much of the same pride the Motoya brother and sister wore as a mantle.

"What is an Irish señor doing in Monterey?" she wanted to know.

"Must you interrogate him?" Carlos demanded. His black eyes flashed. "Where are your manners, Dolores?"

A wave of color washed into the white face. "I am sorry to have been ill-mannered," she said and disappeared toward the house, leaving Carlos and Brit staring after her.

"That one." Carlos snorted much as the horses had done earlier. "Always she slips out, steals my clothes, and rides like a boy." Yet a gleam of pride in his beautiful sister softened his complaint.

With the first decisive move Brit had seen him make, Carlos turned toward the faithful Shamrock, clapped his hands, and told the stable hand that came running, "Care for this horse as if he were your own papa or I will feed you to the dogs." He added when the boy led Shamrock away, "These lazy peons must be made afraid or they do nothing. Come. It is siesta time."

"How old are you, Carlos?" Brit curiously inquired.

"I am a man, señor. Fifteen."

Again Brit hid a grin. "And your sister?"

"Ah, she is eighteen, a woman." Carlos scowled. "Señor, I must tell you. My family will make you welcome. You saved my life." He dramatically placed one hand over the general area of his heart. "I am glad you are not a Yankee. We have much hatred of Yankees. They come, they see, they take our land. Once we had one, two, five haciendas such as this. All are gone, stolen by the intruders who swarm into our land, even though our land grants are hundreds of years old. Were it not for Papa's shrewd nature and the goodness of Dios, God, we would have nothing. Much gold Papa found when others who rushed in found nothing." He snapped his fingers and disposed of those less fortunate.

"We buy back our hacienda, this one." His nostrils flared with hate and a sullen look crossed his normally cheerful face. Then he shrugged. "It it is not good to look back." They walked a few steps in silence then Carlos roused from his memories. "Señor—"

"Call me Brit."

"Brit." Carlos rolled it on his tongue and repeated the name, giving it the Spanish pronunciation until it became *Breet.* "I must give you warning. My sister, Dolores, her name means *sorrows.* She brings sorrow to the boys and men who fall at her little feet. I would not like to see you feel bad when you have been so kind to me, Carlos Montoya."

It had been hard to stifle his mirth earlier. Now it became impossible. Brit laughed until he clutched his sides then wiped his eyes on his sleeve. Seeing the indignation in his young host's face he quickly apologized. "I'm sorry, Carlos. It's just that I've been too busy for girls."

Frank disbelief shone in the dark eyes. "You are how old?"

"Twenty-five."

Carlos swept Brit's tall frame with a wide-eyed stare and threw his hands over his head. "Are there no señoritas in Ireland?"

"We call them colleens. I left Ireland when I was seventeen, after the terrible potato famine."

Comprehension on the boy's face showed him to be knowledgeable of more than California history.

"After we reached America, I worked hard so my family could have a farm."

"Do you have riches?"

"No, Carlos. I worked my way out here."

The dark eyes glistened. "One day I wish to travel and see these great United States, even those where the Yankees live." They had reached the heavy, carved wooden door under the arched overhang that provided a wide porch on all sides of the house. "Enter."

Brit stepped into a new world. No, a world old enough to have been transported intact from Spain. Priceless tapestries, polished dark wood, color and light from casement windows carved with birds and flowers and religious figures.

"*Esta es su casa*. This is your house." Young in years, Carlos didn't fail to give the time-honored greeting to his guest and benefactor. This time Brit had no desire to laugh.

three

Light from a myriad of flickering candles reflected in the highly polished refectory table that rested its impressive length on heavy legs. It danced in Dolores Montoya's black eyes, sparkled mischief into Carlos's face, and dazzled Brit O'Donnell. He had heard of the way the high-caste Spanish lived but it hadn't prepared him for such luxury. The perfume of late-blooming red roses filled the air, along with the spicy scent of Mexican food that burned Brit's throat and made him reach for his tall, crystal water glass.

"A little wine, señor?" Don Carlos, head of the household and an older edition of his fifteen-year-old son, motioned for the servant to fill Brit's glass.

"Thank you, but no." Brit caught the amazed look that went between Carlos and Dolores and set his jaw in a fighting-Irish line. However, his host waved the servant away with an indolent movement of his fine hand. His long, tapered fingers ended in well-tended nails and contrasted strangely with Brit's calloused hands.

"Inez," Don Carlos appealed to his wife. "We owe great gratitude to our guest."

44

The black-clad, slender figure who could easily have passed for her daughter's sister, proudly raised her head. Her dark hair, caught little flames from the candlelight. Brit found himself staring at her as he'd like to do at Dolores but didn't dare. Her voice carried the same liquid sound as Dolores's when she said, "My bad Carlos will ride the devil horse Sol. I am glad you were there, Señor Brit." Genuine thankfulness shone strong in her beautiful face.

"Mama, Sol is no devil horse," Carlos protested hotly. Rich red sprang to his olive cheeks. "Why, even—"

A small disturbance cut short his revelations. "How clumsy of me!" Dolores apologetically sprang to her feet and mopped water from the fluffy white gown set off by a red rose at the neckline, another in her hair.

Keen-eyed Brit saw the warning glance she sent in her brother's direction and bit his lip. So Señorita Montoya had also ridden the white stallion! He marveled that the slim hands could control Sol.

Gold motes twinkled in the girl's dark hair and crept into her eyes when she caught Brit's understanding gaze. An enchanting smile of conspiracy ensured his silence and made his heart thump. Was this why God had led him to California, Brit wondered. This innocent Spanish girl possessed beauty beyond compare. Could she be the mate God wished him to have? Deep color burned in his cheeks.

A startled look replaced the laughter in Dolores's face, almost as if she had divined his thoughts. The next moment she murmured something inaudible and swept from the room, leaving Brit feeling he had been bold and rude. She didn't reappear until the others were almost through the main course and came in so silently that Brit didn't notice until she slid into her highly carved chair. Soft yellow had replaced the white gown. She had been gorgeous in white but was adorable in yellow—and more human. Only her flashing eyes and red roses had kept her from looking like an angel far above the reach of mortal man.

"Tell us about your country," Don Carlos urged. Faultlessly groomed, eyes eager, he leaned forward. So did the others. A thirst for knowledge of the world beyond their own made the Montoyas an excellent audience.

Brit related something of his past, the struggles he and his family had gone through. Once he saw a diamond glisten in Dolores's dark eyes. She hastily brushed it away with an incredibly fine handkerchief edged in lace.

Brit broke off his tale. "Why—"

"What is it, señor?" Carlos asked.

"May I?" He held his hand out to Dolores who drew herself up haughtily. Brit quickly explained, "The lace. It is so different from what we made in Ireland."

"It is the finest Spanish lace," Don Carlos said. "Inez and Dolores have continued the art of lacemaking."

"It's beautiful." Brit examined the handkerchief Dolores handed to him. He went on to tell how the making of lace had saved many from poverty.

Dolores clapped her hands together. "The men? They, too, make lace?"

"Every man, woman, and child old enough to learn made lace. Not so much since we reached America. Father and the boys and I found other work."

"Then you are not wealthy, Señor O'Donnell?" Strange, but coming from Don Carlos it seemed merely a statement rather than prying into a guest's affairs.

Brit shook his head, then his Irish eyes crinkled at the corners. "I have no gold yet God has blessed me with a strong body, a sound mind, and," he paused and glanced around the table, "and with new friends. What more wealth could one ask?"

Was it a shade of disappointment that stole into Dolores's eyes? Did Señora Montoya's eyebrows raise just a trifle?

"Well said," Don Carlos agreed and added, "What is it you do?"

A hearty laugh set the candle flames flickering even more. "I have been a stevedore—that is, I've loaded and unloaded merchandise on the docks. I've rounded up cattle and driven teams and trapped animals for their fur. I've—"

"Been the maker of lace," Dolores audaciously added.

Don Carlos frowned at her before he turned back to Brit. "You need work, now?"

Brit nodded.

Don Carlos tapped his long fingers on the table. "I am in need of a good man," he said slowly. "One who will see that my lazy peons and *vaqueros* work instead of taking siestas while my hacienda is neglected."

Brit wondered why the man didn't see to it himself. His host's next comment answered him.

"I still fight to regain my lands," Don Carlos said. He shrugged. "Even though it is hopeless, I must try. My brother Ramon has been ill. Much of my time has been needed in helping him." With an impatient gesture and a spasm of pain that crossed his features, he rose and shoved back his chair. "Señor O'Donnell, will you do me the honor of becoming my good right hand?"

Brit disciplined a smile at the misquoting of the expression "right hand man," stood and held out his hand. "I will be proud."

Later that night, when he restlessly stood at the deep window in the luxurious room he had been given, Brit looked into the velvety indigo heavens ashine with stars. "Father, I thank Thee for giving me this work. May I do it to Thy glory." A rush of homesickness cut off his low voice. He quickly added, "And if it be that Thou permit, may my family one day find it in their hearts to come to this fertile portion of Thy creation. For Jesus' sake and in His name, Amen."

Life on a Spanish hacienda was not the lazy life some believed, Brit thought one afternoon while overseeing work at the stables. Always the fine horses needed care.

Buildings demanded attention. Gardens had to be cared for, flowers cut and distributed throughout the sprawling house. Dolores did most of the arranging and exquisite bouquets adorned the spacious rooms. Although she was not allowed to enter "Señor Brit's" room, he came in weary each day to the delicate fragrance of blossoms. Carlos said Dolores had a maid deliver them. He winked and added, "Remember what I told you."

Brit ruefully had reason to never forget it! Literally swarms of men and boys haunted the hacienda for a glimpse of the tiny girl-woman. Brit kept his distance. An employee wasn't in the same social strata as those who called, although continued gratefulness on the part of the family kept him from feeling the caste system to any annoying degree. Yet, as fall drifted into a winter unlike any he had ever experienced, Brit knew that no matter how far away he stayed from Dolores, his heart lay in her small, deceptively frail hand...the same hand that could pull Sol and the other horses into obedience.

When had it happened? The moment he discovered the smaller rider was a girl? The sight of a red rose against her snowy gown? The laughter in her eyes, often peeking at him from beneath the wide brim of her sombrero or through a veil when she dressed modestly for an excursion with her mother into nearby Monterey? Surely the look in her eyes could be only for him, he reasoned. Yet, with the next breath, he admitted he knew even less about Spanish señoritas than about sturdy Irish colleens.

At times he longed to confess his love and take his chances. Yet, he held aloof as more weeks faded into the Pacific Ocean at the ending of sunset-glory days.

On the other hand, Brit and Carlos had soon become companions. The restless young *caballero* dogged Brit's heels. He begged to ride Shamrock and goaded him into a race with Sol, who had learned the mastery of an Irishman's touch. He even absorbed some of his new friend's philosophy, although it sorely went against his upbringing.

"But they are only peons!" he protested, when Brit insisted the hacienda workers be treated respectfully and not be spoken to as stable dogs.

"They are men, created in the image of our loving Father," Brit reminded.

Carlos muttered something in Spanish then changed the subject. Yet he, as well as his father, soon noticed how much more willingly their employees followed Brit's direction when the tall man gave it. Neither did they grovel, or scarcely lift their gaze upwards. Brit knew each of them personally. He inquired for the health of their wives and *muchachos*. In turn, they gave him loyalty and good work.

On one point, Brit remained adamant. No matter how often the Montoyas offered wine, he refused. He loved the pure, unfermented grape juice the hacienda afforded but would not touch wine.

"Why?" Carlos prodded one afternoon when they lazed

beneath a giant pine whose gnarled trunk offered a good backrest. Brit had learned that no amount of persuasion could entice his men to forgo the afternoon siesta. He had come to anticipate and enjoy a time of rest before the hacienda again stirred to duty. "Why do you not drink our wine? It is the best in California."

"I would not be for knowing about that," Brit teased.

Carlos snorted and his nostrils pinched.

"It's because I made a vow to God to live soberly and according to His word," Brit told his young friend.

"But our Savior drank wine!" Carlos never dropped an argument until he ran out of plausible ammunition to fuel the disagreement.

Brit sat up straight, clasped his hands around his knees, and stared at the boy he had come to love. "Carlos, I saw those in my country whose children went hungry when their disheartened fathers turned to drink. I'm not saying it was wine, such as you make," he forestalled the other's protest. "But I swore never to touch strong drink. Suppose I did, and one of my brothers saw me, thought it was all right, and followed in my steps? What if he became a drunkard?" Brit shuddered and even Carlos looked sympathetic.

"God once asked a man in the Bible named Cain where his brother was. Cain demanded, 'Am I my brother's keeper?' I believe that everyone who enlists in the army of the Lord is their brother's keeper."

Temporarily silenced by Brit's eloquence, the irrepressible Carlos hushed. But after a few minutes couldn't resist firing a parting shot. "Your brother would never know."

A quiet smile lit up Brit's rugged face. "My friend, God would know and so would I." He stretched, relaxed against the tree, and wordlessly petitioned heaven that he might witness to the rebellious boy and his family.

Christmas as celebrated by the Montoyas and much of Monterey little resembled the modest way the O'Donnells remembered the birth of Christ. Lavish parties and parades with merrymakers in bright costumes, religious icons and statues of the saints blended with the continuing good weather. During that winter of 1858-1859, Brit never saw one snowflake. He liked the bright flowers that bloomed unceasingly yet now and then nostalgically thought of home and how he and the lads and Katie bundled up in old clothes and slid down nearby snowy slopes. He could not join in many of the activities for he did not worship the Montoya way. He learned to stifle the pangs of jealousy that assailed him when Dolores held court for her suitors. Yet seldom did her coquettish face slip from his memory.

Christmas also brought visitors, relatives, and friends who crowded the hacienda to the bursting point. Brit had already met Ramon, a paler, less robust edition of Don Carlos. He gaped open-mouthed when he met Ramon's wife, Mary, with her sad blue eyes and black garb. Every wisp of hair was covered by a mantilla, but her light brows betrayed her heritage.

"Mary Jones, she was," Carlos confided, resplendent in a white suit with gold braid, waiting for yet another festivity to begin. "Uncle Ramon grieved his papa and mama very much by marrying the daughter of a shipowner."

"Then sometimes Castilians do marry outside their own level?" Brit asked.

"Not often." Pity softened the boy's eyes, but a moment later a mischievous look replaced it. "Of course, it does happen—if one can get away from the long nose of the chaperone." With the chameleonlike mood changes that added to his charm, Carlos added, "She always wears black, since the tragedy."

"What tragedy?" Brit noted again the sad light in the blue eyes so unlike the Montoyas.

Carlos shrugged. "It happened before my birth. Their only child. Mama and Papa say they thought Ramon and his wife would go mad. Such a pity."

Even a mysterious tragedy couldn't hold Brit's attention when a soft hand slipped under his arm, a soft voice whispered, "Do you like me. . .my gown, Señor Brit?"

He looked down at Dolores. Her uplifted face and red lips that matched a flower in her hair invited admiration. His heart thudded and gave him courage. "Walk with me in the courtyard and I'll be for telling you if I like you. . .your gown, señorita."

Something in his unusual daring brought a flare of color

to her white skin. She furtively glanced both ways and nodded. Her full, cream skirt swished when they walked toward the open door.

Brit wasted no time. Leaving Carlos standing open-mouthed, he maneuvered Dolores into the courtyard and across to where giant vines and bushes cast deep shadows.

"Well, señor?" She peered up at him. Moonlight sifted through tree branches and dappled her face, leaving her eyes deep, unreadable pools.

"Dolores, *mavourneen*, my heart is filled with love for you. Could you ever care for an Irish lad like me?"

He held his breath and slowly released it when, with a trill of laughter, she asked, "What does *mavourneen* mean?"

"My darling."

"O-oh." Dolores put one hand to her mouth.

He took her free hand and clasped it tightly. "I've never loved a colleen before. You are the first and no heart has ever been for holding love as mine does."

She didn't pull away even when she said, "Papa and Mama would be angry to find me here with you without a chaperone."

He laughed exultantly. "That's why I spoke as I did. There may not be a chance again."

"Señor Brit, I. . .I like you very much, but I must do what Papa says and he will arrange a marriage for me, with one who has lands and gold."

Chagrin and determination mixed in equal parts. "Your

Uncle Ramon followed his heart, Carlos says."

"Y. . .yes, but—"

"Dolores, it is wrong for you to marry unless you love that man with all the love you can give."

"It is the way we live."

Passionate defense rose to his lips, the feeling this night would tell whether he had won or lost in his quest for love. "I have to know. Do you care? I'll not be for asking more than the right to know if I have a chance."

Her proud dark head drooped. "I, too, have not felt this way before."

He gathered the slight form in his arms, raised her chin with one finger, and tenderly kissed her, the first time his lips had touched those of a woman except his mother and sister.

She gasped and pulled away. "Oh, what have I done? I must marry one who will restore the Montoya fortunes. Señor Brit, you must forget this moment," she panted. She stepped into a bright patch of moonlight. "Papa will drive you away if he discovers you. . .I. . .he might even kill you!"

Masterful because of her halting words, Brit stepped into the light, feeling he had truly walked into a light of glory. "Don't you know I will never let you wed another? Dolores, I am young and strong. God will help me. One day I will be rich, rich enough to honorably come to your father and ask for your hand."

A strange look touched her eyes before she said, "Do

you vow to become rich?"

Brit hesitated, reality forcing him to be honest. "I cannot promise great wealth but I believe I can earn enough to make you happy—if you love me as I do you." He added in a burst of impatience, "Can you think that one who has your face before him will not move mountains?"

His impassioned plea hung in the flower-scented air. Dolores slowly gathered up her long skirts with one hand, looked straight into Brit's eyes, and said, "When you do all you have said, return to me."

"Will you be waiting?" he felt compelled to ask.

An incomprehensible smile lifted the corner of her lips. One slender eyebrow raised and she daintily lifted a shoulder. "*Quien sabe*?*" She moved toward the hacienda. "Perhaps ...." Her voice trailed off and Brit stood alone in the courtyard, torn between joy and an unreasoning fear of the future.

*Who knows?

four

Before he confessed his love to Dolores, Brit had known jealousy. Afterwards, it grew worse. Sometimes he ground his teeth when he saw her flirting behind the great fan she wielded like an empress. Even the softening of her dark eyes when she saw him watching couldn't erase his doubts. At times he despaired of ever capturing this Spanish butterfly. He also soberly considered every possible way to keep his promise and bring her riches. So long as he remained on the hacienda, he must stay Señor O'Donnell or Señor Brit, employee, and helplessly stand by while the woman he loved continued her coquettish wiles.

As 1859 wore on, Brit came to a decision. If he were ever to be anything more in the eyes of the Montoyas than friend and right hand to Don Carlos, he must leave and seek his fortune elsewhere. Between tasks and at night, he earnestly prayed.

The answer came in a completely unexpected way, with Carlos bursting into the great dining hall one evening, late to dinner and crying, "News, I have great news. Again we can be rich!" He scarcely paused for breath, but raked his long fingers through his hair until it wildly stood on end.

His dark eyes glistened.

"What is it you are saying?" Don Carlos scowled disapproval of his son's disheveled appearance and half rose.

"Silver! Ledges of silver. . .in the Carson County of western Utah Territory." He spread his arms in an impossibly wide description. "Papa, we must go."

Brit felt his breath quicken. Silver? A rush of blood to his head left him slightly dizzy. He turned toward Dolores.

Eyes ablaze, red lips parted, her hands curled. Triumph twisted her face when she looked at Brit. "Yes, you must go."

He nodded imperceptibly but the others did not notice.

Don Carlos sank back into his chair. "I cannot. My brother Ramon. . .he is not well."

"Then let me go," Carlos pleaded. Excitement glittered in his eyes.

"You?" Don Carlos stared disbelievingly at his son.

"I am a man, Papa." Carlos struck his chest with one arm in the dramatic way Brit had learned to associate with him. "Sixteen, I now am."

Doubt warred with avarice in the older man's face. Suddenly he turned to Brit. "You, señor. Would you be going to look for this treasure?"

"I'd like to." The quiet answer hung in the still air. "It is perhaps the only chance I will ever have to obtain my heart's desire." He refrained from looking at Dolores but could see her rigid posture out of the corner of his eye.

"Would you be willing to take this one?" He waved at Carlos disdainfully.

For once the boy kept silent but his eyes eloquently pleaded.

Brit hesitated. Surely the way would be hard, filled with dangers. He'd read of the fighting and killing in the 1848 Sutter's Mill gold rush, the greed and madness that ended in violence. Yet if it were not for Carlos's warm support, his championing his rescuer and friend, would Dolores have bent from her exalted position enough to notice him?

"I will take him, Señor Montoya." Brit cut short Carlos's shout of joy. "On the understanding that I am to be in control. I'll not be having a lad hurt or. . .or tainted in a mining camp for lack of obedience."

"Do you vow to do this?" Don Carlos demanded.

"By all the saints." Carlos placed his right hand over the general region of his heart.

Brit winced. Swearing by the saints had no part in his faith. Yet he recognized the sincerity of the boy, no, young man's oath. He leveled a look at Carlos. "The moment you break that vow is the moment I will pack you off to home," he warned.

"Si, señor." Carlos let out another whoop. He lifted Dolores from her chair and whirled her about in a wild dance. "I will bring you back riches enough to buy jewels," he babbled. "You can wear them on your fingers and toes and. . . ."

Brit lost the rest. Even in the times of utter hardship, the

O'Donnells had never made money their god as did this unpredictable, warm-hearted family! The hacienda offered more than anyone should want: good food, pleasant surroundings. Flowers wore jewel tones and had gorgeous fragrances. What need for rubies and sapphires or emeralds and diamonds when the whole courtyard supplied blossoms and leaves in the same colors? A little chill shot through him and he turned back toward Dolores. Why must she place such importance on wealth? Her fingers stayed curled into grasping small fists and her eyes betrayed the lust for gold and silver and all that Carlos promised her.

He clamped down hard on the disloyal thought. She had been raised to believe many haciendas and pleasant living were no more than her due. Once he returned with enough to make her comfortable, surely her girlish desires would turn more toward her husband and the home he would provide and away from greed.

Within a few days, Brit and his young companion had gathered together what they would need and prepared to go north and east across the mountains toward the silver strike called the Comstock Lode. Henry Comstock, a prospector, got credit for discovering it although it actually had been found by miners.

Brit managed a quick moment alone with Dolores but it proved to be unsatisfactory. She seemed more interested in the money he would bring back to her than in him or plans for the future. Her enigmatic, *Quien sabe* response to Brit's shy questions about what would happen when he returned left him hollow and troubled.

"What if we don't find the ore?" he bluntly asked.

Fear, disgust, and a visible drawing back accompanied her too quick answer. "Oh, but you will." She pressed his hands in her soft ones, stood on tiptoe, and grazed his cheek with her lips. The stolen caress blotted out doubt and he rode away with its memory warm as the California sun on his face.

There had been an argument about which horse Carlos should ride. "It must be Sol," he insisted. "The white stallion is a fit mount for a Montoya."

For once, Brit lost patience with his peacock strutting. "The last thing you need in a mining camp is to have it known you are from a wealthy family," he said sharply. "How long do you think Sol would escape the greedy hands of those who will pour into Carson County as we are doing?"

"But you're riding Shamrock!" Carlos sulked.

"Shamrock is a good horse but not a fine or race horse," Brit retorted. "Now choose an animal that won't be conspicuous." He eyed Carlos's lavish clothes with distaste. "And leave all the black and silver stuff here." He strode to his room and returned with an awkwardly tied bundle. "Wear these." The wrappings fell back and disclosed rough pants, shirt, sheep-lined jacket, and scuffed dandy-sized boots.

"Señor!" Carlos jerked back, insulted. "I, Carlos Montoya, to wear those garments? Never!"

"Fine. Then I'll head out alone." Brit stooped to gather the scorned clothes but a slim hand stopped him.

"Carlos will wear what you say." Pale-faced and resolute, Dolores glared at her brother. "Have you so soon forgotten your vow to the saints?"

Protest died aborning. Carlos grabbed the bundle, ran out, and soon came back, transformed from proud *caballero* to a reasonable facsimile of a *vaquero*. A few hours later, at Brit's insistence, he agreed to ride a black gelding named King, seated in the plainest saddle the hacienda afforded.

Oddly enough, once the two left Monterey, Carlos's rebelliousness fell away. He reveled in sleeping out, thrived on the rough camp fare Brit provided, and proved to be far more than the spoiled scion of Castilian stock. In an amazingly short time, he also became adept at caring for King, fetching firewood, building fires, and repacking supplies. His riding and roping were, of course, superb.

"I never knew how good life could be," he told Brit one night after a long ride. "Do you think we will find silver? Or gold?"

"If God permits."

"Why do you always say such things?" he curiously asked, flat on his back with his head propped against a saddle.

"Because they are true." Brit's gaze rested on the dark head.

"When I was just a *muchacho,* I said my prayers to Señor God," Carlos remarked in the sleepy stillness when even the birds had gone to roost. He sighed. "But God did not save our other haciendas."

"If it hadn't been for Him, perhaps you wouldn't still own the hacienda at Monterey," Brit quietly told him.

Carlos lay prone for a long time, then whispered, "Perhaps." A few minutes later his even breathing showed that he slept.

Brit did not. A host of memories and doubts settled over him like a storm cloud. Could he and Dolores ever find real happiness, coming from such different backgrounds? If not, why had it seemed clear that God had led him to Monterey? He closed his eyes and a hundred images of the girl he loved danced before him. Dolores, peeping over her great fan. Dolores, pure as the angels in her white gown and opening red rose. Dolores, whose lips had trembled at his kiss but whose hands clenched in greed. Which picture represented the true person? Before Brit could decide, they merged and blended until sleep swept them away with a single stroke. Yet his dreams tugged and pulled, until he felt like a swimmer who could no longer fight against raging waters but must go down.

The journey required stamina almost beyond Carlos's

strength. At times the mountains and canyons loomed, each an obstacle to overcome. Brit's deep love and admiration for his friend grew. At times Carlos's hands shook with fatigue, yet he never complained. At other times, fear shone in the dark eyes when the riders followed a narrow trail along the edge of a cliff where one false step by King or Shamrock would send them plunging hundreds of feet to their deaths on rocks below. Brit taught Carlos to watch out for soft earth ready to slide, loose rocks poised to launch an avalanche, trails eaten away by flood and rain.

One afternoon they reached what looked to be an impassable stretch of path across a steep shale hillside and Brit hesitated.

"Señor Brit, do we cross that?" Carlos pointed to the gray white expanse between them and the trees beyond.

Brit had grown used to the fact that no matter how often he told Carlos to simply call him Brit, it did not come natural to the young man. Now he eyed the hundred yards before them. "If we don't cross here, it means backtracking for miles." Yet he doubtfully viewed the shale. "I think we will be safe if we go easy." He prodded Shamrock with his boot heels and urged him forward. The bay gelding snorted and gingerly stepped forward.

"Allow me to go first," Carlos suggested, even while fear rested in his whitened face. "I do not weigh so much. Should I fall, you can catch me with your rope."

"Are you sure?" Brit didn't like the idea but it made sense.

"Si. King will leave footprints and Shamrock can follow." Carlos didn't wait for consent but swung King around past Brit and Shamrock. Sure-footed as a mountain goat, King picked his way across. From the other side, Carlos shouted. His white teeth gleamed and he slid from the saddle then tied King to a nearby evergreen.

"What are you doing?" Brit hollered.

Carlos removed his lariat from King's saddle. "If you slide, I, Carlos Montoya, will catch you."

Brit chuckled but humored him by not stepping out onto the shale until Carlos had his lariat coiled and ready. He had learned how deeply pride was ingrained into the lad. Now he guided Shamrock into the trail King had blazed and headed across the bad spot.

All went well for the first fifty yards. Then something, probably a loosening of the hillside from Shamrock's movement, caused a quiver of earth beneath the faithful horse's feet. He shied, then tried to speed up and get away from the sliding shale. Brit realized the time for caution had passed. Unless they could cover the remaining distance pronto, he and Shamrock would end up at the bottom of the long hill, buried in the shale that already gathered momentum.

"Go, Shamrock!" Brit leaned forward, urging the horse ahead.

With a loud whinny, the bay tried to leap. He could not. His hooves sank into the moving ground. A heartbeat later, Brit felt the inevitable downward pull of the landslide they had created! An involuntary prayer of thanks that Carlos stood safe on the other side rose in his heart, then, "God, help me!"

Zing.

Had God made sure the single chance for Carlos's throw? In any event, his lariat sang in the air, settled over Shamrock's head, and tightened. A quick glance showed Carlos expertly backing black King, rope tight around the saddle horn.

"Now, Shamrock!" Again Brit sank heels into his mount's heaving sides.

With a great pulling together of muscles followed by a spring, the range-trained horse responded. The pressure of the rope and steady pull toward safe ground blended with Shamrock's struggles. Inch by inch they moved, fighting the ever-increasing shifting shale, until Shamrock's hooves reached stable earth. He scrambled onto firm ground seconds before the whole hillside slid to the valley floor with a mighty roar, leaving a naked, scarred patch of slope.

Brit tumbled from the saddle. Sweat streaked Carlos's face and the horses' flanks. Brit felt cold perspiration crawl beneath his shirt. "Wisha, wisha,*" he whispered.

"Señor Brit," Carlos breathed. "We will not return this way, I think."

Brit stared at his rescuer, whose eyes were wide pools of relief. Laughter bubbled inside him and spilled over. He threw himself on the needle-covered ground and roared until memory of the near tragedy asserted itself into

*an Irish expression of surprise

his mind and stilled his mirth. He stood, started to hold out his hand to Carlos, then abandoned the formality and dropped a hard arm over the younger man's shoulders. "Gracias, Carlos."

"Si." Some of the other's insouciance returned. His eyes sparkled. "You save me, I save you."

"And thanks be to God we're standing here talking about it," Brit reminded, before turning away to hide the Irish mist in his eyes. "Let's see if we can find a stream or lake or something. I can still taste dust." He remounted Shamrock, waited until Carlos clambered aboard King, then led off on the faint trail. His lips twitched and he glanced back. "You were right about one thing. We won't be for coming back this way!"

Once across the range of mountains, their way led down. They discovered a blue jewel lake with water so icy their teeth chattered when they drank. King and Shamrock drank deeply then splashed in, eager to rid themselves of the day's soil. Brit followed suit. So did Carlos. But long before the horses snorted and came back out of the water the two men shivered in front of a roaring fire. They also took the opportunity to don fresh clothing and wash and dry their traveling clothes.

Fed, warmed, nearly asleep, Brit surprised them both by impulsively asking, "Carlos, do you honestly think your sister would marry me?" His hopes and heart sank at the long, thoughtful silence between them before Carlos replied.

"Perhaps, if we carry riches to her from our journey."

"Would you marry a poor girl if you loved her very much?" Brit couldn't help asking.

"Si." This time the answer came back with the speed of a hummingbird's wings. "But for my sister it is different."

"Why?"

Carlos shrugged. "She is a woman."

All Brit's protests ended against the wall of tradition embodied in the four words that sounded a death knell in his heart. So had Dolores been trained, so would she obey. Even if she loved Brit to distraction, she must marry one who would restore the family fortunes, Carlos said.

"Do you think that is right?" Sleepiness gone, Brit leaped to his feet and paced the ground in front of the fire.

"I never thought about it at all until you came," Carlos admitted. "Besides. . . ." He poked at the fire with a long stick. The end caught and blazed up, casting light on his earnest face. "Dolores could never be happy if she were poor."

"I suppose you consider anyone poor who doesn't have at least one large hacienda, fine horses, and many servants," Brit said bitterly.

"Señor Brit, I believe you are the richest man I have ever known." Carlos stood and faced him. "Since we left Monterey many days ago I have watched you lift your face to the night sky. I have seen the stars and moon shine in your eyes and how you watch the sun get up and go to bed, wearing its coat of many colors. I have seen you bow your head against the storm." He swallowed convulsively and his voice turned ragged.

"This day, when I made my loop and sent it to save you, I saw your face. If the rope missed, you would die. Señor, I saw no fear! Your lips moved. I knew you talked to your God. You are young, in love with Dolores, eager to live and find silver so you may ask for her hand." His voice faltered and broke.

Even so, Brit wasn't prepared for Carlos's final burst of oratory that allowed him to look into his companion's heart. In liquid tones, so low Brit strained to hear the words, came wonder.

"With all this, I saw peace, Señor, a man who has courage and peace and. . .faith, what need has he of silver and gold?"

Stunned by the revelation of Carlos's challenge, Brit turned from him and strode into the forest until he could find solitude to deal with his warring emotions—and accept the magnitude of being a witness to Carlos Montoya of the living God Who gave peace the world could not understand.

five

Angus McFarlane's fears about losing the child he found in the desert proved groundless. During the ten happy years following the richest discovery he could ever make, the grizzled man and young girl periodically returned to the spot marked with the cairn of stones where Angus had buried the man who carried Joyous. Only once did they find horse tracks and they had been there for months, so told no desert tales.

True to his promise, the desert wanderer forsook his travels, settled down with his adopted daughter on a small place in southern California, and turned Jenny out to pasture. He hired a combination housekeeper-companion-teacher for Joy with the gold they'd found at Sutter's Mill and watched the pretty child grow into a charming woman.

Joy never lost the reddish gold cast to her hair or the dozen or so freckles across her nose that shone gilt in the hot sunlight. Her laughing blue eyes could darken with thought or from seeing anyone unjustly treated. More than once she had driven tormentors away from persecuting a puppy or kitten, using nothing more than her flashing, magnificent eyes and scornful words that cowed bullies even while they admired her. Woe to those who treated others in any way other than the Golden Rule that Angus had taught her from the *Auld Book*.

All good things must end. So did Angus and Joy's idyllic existence. Twinges he ignored until he could no longer do so, drove Angus to a doctor. The verdict—a tricky heart that could go on beating steadily for a year or two at the most.

Never had he suffered such anguish. To leave Joyous? "God," he prayed in his bed chamber that night, gaze fixed on the low-hanging stars visible through his wide-open window. "Grant that Thy servant may see her cared for before Thou calls me."

All night his lips repeated the prayer and with dawn came peace—and a decision. Little remained of the gold they had found. It hadn't particularly mattered until now. Their place furnished fruit and vegetables. A few cows and chickens gave butter, cheese, milk, meat, and eggs. Joy bartered them for sugar and flour at a small nearby store. At her insistence, the woman who cared for her until she grew tall and strong was now just a memory and Joy ran their little household and sweetly ordered Angus around with efficiency.

Once he left her, she couldn't live there alone. Angus didn't trust some of the men who, with any encouragement, would pitch a tent on the McFarlane doorstep. His innocent daughter had so far shown no interest in even the nicest but Angus must not leave her to shift for herself.

Heart beating unevenly, he looked up from the flapjacks, bacon, and golden-yolked eggs at breakfast and said, "Joyous, I'm hankering to go prospecting again."

A little flush crept into her smooth cheeks. Her eyes sparkled. "When? Where?" She clapped her hands together. "What fun it will be! It's been a long time since we went into the desert." A little frown puckered her brow. "You gave up your wandering for me, Daddy. Are...are you sorry?"

"You know better than that."

The gentle reproach brought laughter back to her face. "I can be ready tomorrow. So can Jenny." She sighed. "I'm glad we'll always have a Jenny. I remember how I cried when the one who first carried me after you found me died from getting out and into some loco weed. I love the new one, too, though. Tell me where we're going."

Angus inwardly sighed with relief. So far, he hadn't had to mention his heart. Someday he would have to tell her but not now. Not until God could show the way for him to ensure Joy's future security. "In the west-central part of Utah Territory, Carson County, there's been a strike of rich ore—silver, some gold. My fingers are just itching to get back to prospecting and mining, lass. Are ye with me?" In times of deep emotion he reverted to his Scottish speech.

"Why, of course." Her eyes opened wide and her reddish gold brows went up. Her curly golden lashes intensified the blue of her eyes. Joy glanced around the small but cozy room. "We won't. . .will we sell our place here?"

Angus had already thought of that. He sensed that because of her unusual past she needed somewhere to come back to when her wandering stopped. Now he quickly shook his head. "Nay. Our neighbor's grown son is wanting to work the land. He can live here while we're gone and keep all he can grow."

She sprang to her feet. Her blue-and-white checked dress beneath her white apron swished around her dainty ankles. "Daddy, I am so glad that of all the people in the world, God let it be you who found me." She pressed a quick kiss to the top of his whitening head and fled, but not before Angus saw the shine of tears.

His heart throbbed, not from pain, but from knowledge of what Joyous would suffer after his death. Again he prayed that God might extend his life and help him prepare Joy for the time to come.

With the future in mind, Angus forced himself to put reticence aside. On the journey north and east to the Comstock Lode, a dozen times he planted seeds to bear fruit when he no longer would be there to see it. "We've had good years together, lass, but one day ye'll be wanting a home of your own and a laddie who'll take care of ye."

Her meadowlark trill of laughter gladdened his heart and turned his thin lips up in a sympathetic smile. "Don't tell me you're trying to get rid of me, after all this time," she pleaded in mock fear, then spoiled her dramatics with another laugh. "Besides, haven't you taught me that when the laddie I'm to love comes, I will know it?"

"Aye." Angus kept his gaze fixed on the trail ahead but his mouth twitched.

"I wonder what he will be like," the girl mused. A dreamy look crossed her expressive features. "Tall and thin like John, the farmer? Sturdy and homely but good all the way through like Edward? Dark with the flashing eyes of Juan?" She shrugged daintily and the shoulders of her riding clothes moved in a show of disinterest. "Why think about him—this laddie—until he appears?"

Angus had no answer for her without disclosing the possible short time before their separation until reunited in heaven.

Another time he warned, "When we get to the mining camp, I want ye to wear the heavy gray veil I bought for ye to keep off dust on the trail. Canna ye remember how 'twas at Sutter's Mill?"

She nodded vigorously and the fat braid she wore while traveling bounced. "Men yelling and noise, noise, noise." She grimaced. "I don't look forward to that."

"We'll try to locate far enough away from the boom town so we can have a bit of quiet," he promised. Compelled by curiosity and driven by dread, he asked, "Joy, s'pose that something happened to me? What would you do?"

Her shock told him he'd introduced a totally new idea. "Why, what do you mean?" Fear paled her cheeks.

He fumbled. "Well, in a mining camp, a body's never sure what kind of folks will be there and accidents do happen." He felt like a liar although every word spoken was certainly true and represented the hidden dangers of where they would be.

Joy thought for a long time before she said, "I don't know. I guess first I'd cry then ask God to help me. He would, you know."

The quiet assurance in her voice repaid him for all the hours Angus had spent teaching her the truths of the Bible. A load of worry slipped from his shoulders. With faith such as hers, he need have little concern. "Aye," he agreed and turned her attention to an inquisitive gopher who peered at them with bright eyes then popped back into his hole.

By the time Angus and Joyous reached Carson County, Virginia City had already shot up like a mushroom. Crude buildings and tents stood on yellow earth 6500 feet high in the Sierra Nevada Mountains, close to Mount Davidson and the famous Comstock Lode. Stories of how a person could pass through a town composed of a half-dozen tents in the morning and return to a mile-long strip of tent saloons booming with business ran rampant. Dugouts and shacks, sometimes built of packing cases or rocks, littered the ugly area whose claim to beauty lay in rolling, sparsely covered hills that gave way to blue, snow-capped mountains in the distance.

The McFarlanes had reason to rejoice over the small remaining hoard of gold their simple living had left them. The price of provisions soared almost as high as the mountains. Joy gasped, set her chin in a firm line, and decided to plant a small vegetable garden as soon as possible. Virginia City had no wood or water; it had to be hauled in from nearby hamlets springing up in the area. Food hauled in from California over the mountains sold at the asking price.

Angus managed to find a tiny piece of land away from the sprawling shacks and tents. With Joy's able help, he built a two-room shelter, crude but snug. Joy papered the walls with layers of newspaper to add extra warmth. She also observed Angus's warning and wore the heavy gray veil any time she went where she could be seen. Even so, she felt the bold gaze of ruffians who seemed to have more time to lounge in the open-flapped tent saloons than be out mining.

Her cheeks burned one afternoon when she made a natural mistake and approached a woman standing before a counter made of planks resting on heavy boxes in a dry goods establishment. "How nice to see another woman here!" she exclaimed, admiring the rich deep blue of the other's enveloping cloak.

The woman turned. Joy gasped. No friendliness warmed the hard, painted face. When the blue cloak slipped, it exposed white neck, shoulders and some of the voluptuous woman's bosom. "Sorry, girlie, we ain't the same type." Amusement and a lifted eyebrow reduced Joy to small-girl status and left her staring open-mouthed, and glad for the gray veil.

"Sorry, miss," the harried storekeeper apologized. "She's not for the likes of you to be greetin'." He leaned across the counter, glanced both ways and whispered, "Decent folks oughta run her kind out of town, along with the sharpie gamblers and those who sell booze day and night."

Joy mumbled something and beat a hasty retreat, only to stop short with her first step to the dusty street. A crowd had gathered at the far end. One man wildly gesticulated, his hands going like windmills in a tornado. Another shook his head violently. His, " 'Tain't so" reached the appalled girl. Sickened by the dust, noise, and heat, Joy slipped through the crowd, back to a quieter street and quickly made her way out of town and to the haven of the tiny shack she and Angus called home.

Should she tell him what happened? She considered then slowly shook her head. What good would it do? For some reason he thought they should stay until they could strike it rich, or at least find enough ore to build up their dwindling resources. She must not tell how she hated everything about their new life. Gone were the days when she happily tended her garden and cows and chickens. How could she grow things in this place when barrels of water could only be obtained for exorbitant prices? She couldn't depend on rainfall to water the plants for her. Discouragement drooped her shoulders and she wearily walked on.

A few weeks later, Angus came home grimy but chuckling. He washed up, being as sparing of the precious water as possible, then sat down to supper. "Lass, I heard a tale today." Many times he started out with those words.

Lifted from her lassitude, Joy smiled and waited. One of the few good things about this place lay in the stories.

"Seems that a couple of men needed a place to hole up for the winter last fall so they built a shelter, using all the rocks they could find." Angus chuckled again and his gray eyes almost closed with mirth. "When spring came, those two were in for a big surprise. The rocks they'd piled up for walls turned out to be high-grade silver ore! According to the story, that shelter turned out to be worth seventy-five thousand dollars!"

"Really?" Joy's fork clattered against the tin plate they used when wandering.

"Aye." Angus took a big bite out of a biscuit. "Now, I wonder if when fall comes we should make us a rock house!"

Joy didn't tell him she hoped that by fall they would have a tidy amount gleaned from his findings so they could go home.

Among the hordes who flocked in after wealth, one couple came for a different harvest—souls. The day Reverend Mills and his bustling, buxom wife hit Virginia City began a new era for Joy, who had been driven to distraction by her surroundings and idleness. Keeping her home neat, preparing meals, and shopping for what little they could afford left too many empty hours. Her nimble fingers had long since mended clothes and even the struggle to keep them washed didn't take up enough of her time. Late one afternoon, a noise outside changed all that.

She cautiously peeked out before opening the door wide to the thin-faced man who wore a clerical collar and rode a dilapidated horse. "Miss McFarlane? The storekeeper told me you and your father lived up here. I'm Reverend Mills."

"Step down and come in," she welcomed eagerly. "You're the first company we've had."

"I won't be the last." Saddle leather creaked when he slid off the nag and walked stiffly toward her. "My wife is eager to call but we felt I should come first to see if. . . ."

She knew he silently added, *if she'd be welcome* or *if this is a fit place for a lady*. A dimple showed when she said, "Not every place is suitable for a call from a minister's wife." She ushered him inside and reached for the precious hoard of tea she'd been saving.

Reverend Mills shook his head. "None for me, thanks. Betsy will have an early supper waiting for me." He put aside his small talk and went straight to the point. "Miss McFarlane, I see you are a Christian."

Her gaze followed his to the open Bible on a nearby table made from a box. "Oh, yes. Daddy Angus taught me about Jesus from the time he found me."

The minister's eyebrows raised. "Found you? Why, aren't you his daughter?"

"His adopted daughter." Joy's eyes shone like twin mountain lakes in sunlight. She briefly related her past, mentioning she couldn't remember before the terrifying time in the desert when the man who later died carried her.

"How old are you?" Reverend Mills wanted to know.

Her laughter rippled. "Daddy says I'm sixteen or seventeen or eighteen, he doesn't know which."

The minister joined in her laughing. "What is your name?"

"Joyous."

"What a beautiful name! Do you remember where you got it?"

"Daddy Angus said when he asked me who I was I said 'J-yes.' So he called me Joyous."

"Hmm. You could have meant Joyce."

"That's what Daddy said, but by the time he thought of it, we were used to Joyous. Besides, he usually calls me Joy."

"Joyce is actually Latin for *joyous* so you are well-named," he told her, then smiled. "I must be going but Betsy will call soon." He started for the door and paused. "Miss McFarlane. . .Joyous. . .do you sing?"

"Of course." She smiled at him. "Daddy Angus and I sing hymns when we travel. At home, too."

"Praise God! Betsy and I felt we must come to this godless camp and share the good news of the Gospel of our

Lord. We both sing a little but if we can find a few others who will lift their voices in song, it will add to our meetings. Many a sinner has been touched by a hymn when he wouldn't listen to a sermon. Child, are you willing to help us see if we can drown out a little of the wicked roar of this place with righteous songs instead of the vile, bawdy music of the streets?"

"Oh, yes." Joy felt excitement stir within her. She followed Reverend Mills out to his excuse for a horse and called after him, "I can hardly wait to meet your wife."

"You'll like her," he promised and rode off with a wave, leaving Joy happier than she had been for weeks.

She did like Mrs. Mills, who arrived promptly at two the next afternoon, astride the sorry horse.

"Call me Betsy," she said, even before she clambered down and came into the shack. Her sharp eyes in her round face surveyed the tidy surroundings and she plumped onto a box chair on which Joy had placed a pillow. "Glad to see you've made the most of what you have. Never could abide those who whine and say there's no use trying to keep a shack clean. Chances are, they wouldn't keep a place clean if they had a mansion." Her tongue ran as if well-oiled, but not an unkindly thing did she say. Instead, she brought cheer and happiness to the lonely girl.

"Now, come Sunday, we're going to have a meeting. No use waiting, I told my husband. I brought a list of songs—

do you know them?" She handed Joy a piece of brown wrapping paper of dubious origins. On it were penciled: *Amazing Grace*; *All Hail the Power of Jesus' Name*; *Oh, For a Thousand Tongues to Sing*; *Blest Be the Tie that Binds*; *Holy, Holy, Holy*; *Come Thou Almighty King*; *O God, Our Help in Ages Past*; and *Abide With Me*.

"Oh, I forgot to put down *How Firm a Foundation*," Betsy said. "Do you know it?"

"Yes, and the others, too," Joy gladly told her.

"Good." Betsy's face wreathed in smiles. "Will that father of yours agree to sing with us?"

"He already has." Mischief twinkled in the girl's eyes and her gilt freckles shone. "He is quite shy but I just told him if ever people needed to hear the old hymns it had to be Virginia City and he reluctantly agreed."

"Well, that's settled. First meeting or two the four of us may be the only ones who know the songs but folks'll soon catch on. Besides," she added shrewdly, "my husband says some of the decent ones are glad enough to have something to go to besides the Sunday horse racing, even if 'tis a preaching."

six

Sunday. The lone day of the week when exhausted miners put aside their tools for other pursuits. Some washed clothes. Some wrestled or raced their horses. Others read the Bible. They were the ones who smiled when the unaccustomed sound of a rousing hymn issued from a large tent Reverend Mills had erected at the edge of town. Another hymn followed, calling the devout and curious alike to the new phenomenon. The storekeeper occupied a front row seat constructed of long planks resting on wooden packing boxes. One by one, rough men took their places, sometimes stumbling from embarrassment when they saw the pure, beautiful face of Joyous McFarlane turned their way and smiling.

Reverend Mills preached a message of salvation designed to pierce hearts. The harmony of the Mills-McFarlane quartette added its invitation and brought back long-forgotten memories of home and church to those who had wandered away. Every person who attended left touched—many by the message, all by the girl who shone in her crude surroundings like a white flower in a coal field. Her clear voice had never before been used for the Lord and when she sang one stanza alone of *Abide With*

Me tears sprang to more than one pair of eyes.

"Next week there will be more," the storekeeper promised, excitement filling his face. "Word will get around, just wait and see." He confidentially added for Reverend Mills's ear alone, "Even those who patronize the saloons on Saturday night might be drawn here—by the girl."

The good reverend drew himself up indignantly and Betsy, whose keen ears missed nothing, retorted, "If they come for that reason they might as well stay away."

"Not so," the storekeeper protested. "Once they get here they'll get a good dose of religion. What's the harm of using honey to catch flies, er, the souls of men?"

"Just you keep your lip buttoned," Betsy warned. "I'll not have that girl bothered by the likes of miserable sinners who put on a good front so's to gain her friendship."

He nodded, but trotted back to his quarters behind his store with a grin. Say what she liked, it wouldn't keep the men of Virginia City away, not from that girl, no siree. No wonder she had been swathed in the gray veil when she came to town.

Now that she had the Reverend and Betsy Mills and singing and church, along with midweek prayer meeting, Joy could stand the primitive conditions.

Angus said nothing to anyone except her, but quietly carried out his work and with success. While he found no ledges of silver such as rumor put out were everywhere in the area, a steady stream of small pockets of gold, silver-bearing rock, and, now and then, a gold nugget furnished their living and the beginning of a cache. Wise in the ways of greedy men, the canny Scotsman hid the gold in a well-concealed hole at the foot of his shack next to a corner post where he could add to the store when necessary. The discoveries of the silver posed a problem. He could hardly pack out great sections of rock and, if he announced the find, claim jumpers and unscrupulous mine owners alike would rush in.

"What we need is someone we can trust who has the money to develop this latest discovery," Joyous sighed one evening after Angus announced he had literally stumbled over what might be a rich vein of ore. He showed her a piece he had chipped off in the spot miles from town and away from most of the other miners.

"Aye." He fingered the sample of ore.

"We can trust the storekeeper and the Millses but they don't have enough money," she went on. "Those who do, I wouldn't trust as far as I could throw a pick and shovel."

"Aye."

Impatient with his brief responses she still couldn't help giggling. "I wonder what Reverend Mills would say if I stood up in meeting and asked God to send a rich, honest man."

The sometimes dour Scot's gray eyes twinkled and he threw his head back and laughed. "The reverend would be shocked but Mrs. Betsy would probably say 'Amen.'"

Joy could just picture it. When she stopped laughing she gasped, "Well, we're supposed to make known to our

Father those things we need."

"Aye." Angus reverted to his usual taciturn self but his gaze followed her adoringly when she caught up a light shawl and announced she planned to walk a little before dark. "Don't go far," he warned. "We never know what beastie might be lurking near, four-legged or two."

"Two-legged!" She turned a startled face toward him.

"Aye. Ye are getting uncommonly handsome, lass. The laddies and some not so young have already approached me, seeking your hand. 'Twas better while ye wore the veil, I'm thinking."

"As if I've seen anyone here I'd marry." Joy dismissed the suggestion with a wave of her hand. "Why, I scarcely know any boys or men except for the storekeeper and—" She broke off and color flared in her cheeks. "He wasn't one of them, was he?"

Angus shook his head and chuckled. "Nay, but 'twouldn't surprise me if he should." He cocked his head to one side, scanned her as if deciding whether to speak, and finally added, "Don't take on airs but a mine owner old enough to be your daddy vowed to bestow the value of your weight in silver on us should I but put in a good word for him."

Shock imprisoned her tongue for a moment. Then angry red streaked her neck and face above the blue-and-white checked dress she wore so often.

"Lass." A timbre in Angus's voice she'd never heard before silenced the building protest inside her. "Ye are the only decent girl or woman in Virginia City so far, except for Mrs. Betsy." He struggled with words and she realized how hard it was for him to speak.

"Even men who. . .who seek the other kind bow before your innocence. Virginia City has more than a lust for gold and silver. A madness sometimes comes to men who are away from homes and families." Dull red suffused his worn face. "Ye are safe from harm because everyone here knows that should a wretch threaten you in any way he would swiftly be brought to justice."

Joy shuddered, thinking of the growing number of those in Boot Hill.

"Just never open the door to a stranger," Angus went on. "Those who are coming in won't know the rough code this brawling place still abides by and any danger would be from those."

"But won't our Father protect me?" Joy's eyes dilated with fear at the revelations.

"Aye, and yet we canna always understand His ways. Sometimes He permits bad things to happen. The sun rises and He 'sendeth rain on the just and the unjust,' the *Auld Book* tells us in Chapter Five of Matthew." He reflected for a moment. "Don't be afraid. Just be canny. Now run along for your bit of a walk."

Joy soberly stepped outside, but she didn't go far. She couldn't help being frightened, although all the times they had traveled in the desert, mountains, or valleys her fearlessness had given her peace. Or had it been faith in God and Angus? She paced back and forth in front of their crude home and thought about many things she had taken for granted. How still it was, away from the town, whose lights twinkled below her. From it rose the evening din she remembered from the rare times she and Angus had been here at night, mercifully dimmed by distance.

Her soul revolted within her and she cried aloud, "God, why must those You created be like this? Toiling and moiling, little recognizing or caring for You?" Sickened by what Angus had told her, her voice broke. "Please, we need someone to help us mine the silver. As soon as we can satisfy this strange urge within Angus that is so unlike him, we'll leave here." Yet the tired faces of the Millses' rose to haunt her. If she and Angus weren't here, could the reverend and Betsy carry on? Without vanity she knew her voice drew ever larger numbers to the tent, filling the benches and spilling out into the dusty street. Some had confessed their sins and asked the Lord into their hearts. They encouraged rough comrades to do the same and yet lawlessness prevailed, fights ended in death, and the number of rowdies and gunmen far outshone the "church crowd" as one resentful saloon owner who feared a loss of business called them.

Joy still wore the gray veil when she went to town but lifted it once inside the store. With new awareness after her talk with Angus, she noticed things she had overlooked before. The way the men glanced at her, shuffled their feet, and looked away. Whispers, "That's the red-headed gal who sings at church." Doors to business places quickly opened by bowing men. She wisely held her head high and didn't let on there had been a change in her knowledge. Yet she dreaded a time that seemed inevitable.

One afternoon Joy stayed longer at Betsy's than she had planned. She started toward home and got out of town safely but a half-mile from home, on the sloping hillside she must climb, a furtive rustling in the sparse brush along the way sent her heart shooting to her throat.

"Who's there?" she called, forcing her voice to steadiness.

The noise stopped.

She walked on, breathing hard from the upward turn and her increased speed. The brush moved.

Anger replaced her touch of fear. "Whoever you are, come out of there this instant!"

Again the noise stopped, but a gentle bray and a shaggy gray brown head that poked out of the growing darkness brought a gasp of relief.

"Jenny, what are you doing here?" She put her arms around her burro friend's neck and rubbed her cheek against Jenny's nose, then picked up the dangling lead rope and led the trotting burro toward home. Worry consumed her. Jenny shouldn't be loose and wandering. Had something happened to Daddy Angus? Fear lent speed and she scrambled up the last of the hill and ran across the open space to the cabin. "Daddy?"

"Here, lass."

Gladness washed through her. A voice so strong

couldn't come from one hurt or sick.

Angus appeared in the doorway. "I grew concerned and sent Jenny to meet ye." His quick glance betrayed that concern. "It's not like ye to be late."

"I wasn't paying attention to the time," she told him and gave the old man a quick hug before turning her attention back to the burro. "My rescuer almost scared me to death by loitering in the brush looking for food instead of staying on the trail." She tied Jenny, lovingly scolded her, and brought a handful of precious oats along with a bucket of water.

In spite of promises and determination not to be caught in the dark again, a few days later Joy found herself in the same predicament.

"Wait for the reverend," Betsy advised. "He can take you home."

Joy thought of how tired he was when he got in from his visiting those located for miles around and how his nag looked even more tired. "I'll be all right," she assured her friend. "Daddy will send Jenny for me." She told about what had happened a few nights earlier, while tying on her veil and preparing to leave. They shared a good laugh and Joy set out for home.

About the same place she had encountered Jenny the other time she heard a familiar rustle of bushes.

"You can't fool me, you wretch! Come out of there," she called. She heard a funny sound, a drawing in of breath. "Come on, will you? We have to get home?"

Her blood froze when a dark-eyed, dark-haired youth stumbled into the path before her, clutching a bloodstained shoulder of his coat with his right hand. "Si, señorita."

A heartbeat later he collapsed at her feet.

What should she do? Thoughts raced like locomotives through her mind. All of Angus's warnings rose to attack her. Yet the pleading look in the pain-filled eyes, clear even in the increasing darkness, and the faint memory of familiar words Angus had read to her about those who passed by a wounded Samaritan overrode caution. She dropped to her knees, shook the uninjured right arm. "Who are you? What happened?"

He roused enough to utter but one word, *"Bandidos."*

Bandidos. Bandits, common to the area. Why would they attack a lad who looked even younger than she? "What does it matter?" she fiercely told herself. She slipped her hand under the stained coat. It came away slippery and smelling of blood. Joy forced the boy's right hand away, yanked open the coat and shirt, and recoiled at the hole in the fleshy part of his shoulder. She bit her lip, reached for her petticoats, and rapidly tore a great length from the bottom. Half became a pad, the other half she bound over the pad and around his upper arm.

He stirred, looked at her from great black gulfs of pain, and tried to speak.

"Don't talk," she ordered sharply. "I'll go for help." Thank God she had been late this night! Joy gathered up her skirt and mutilated petticoats and ran the rest of the way home panting for breath. She burst into the shack. "Daddy, come quick, I—" Her voice failed. Her eyes opened wide with shock.

A man lay prone on the floor in a pool of blood that seeped from his head. Angus bent over him, anger, grief, and worry etched into the furrows of his face.

"Who—what—?"

"He's been shot. The bullet didn't go deep but he's lost too much blood. I canna say if he will live." Angus's gaze shot to Joy. His eyes became slits. "Lass, ye have blood on your hands!"

"A young man, a boy, really," Joy breathlessly told him. "Shot through the left shoulder. I bandaged him as best I could and came to get you."

"Did ye stanch the blood?"

"Yes." Again she bit her lip to steady herself.

"Then we must care for this lad first." Angus dropped to his knees. "Get me the whiskey. 'Twill burn like fire, so it's good our visitor's not awake."

She ran for the bottle never used for drink but always available for medicinal purposes. "Where did you find him?"

"On our doorstep. He and the young one must be pardners."

"The boy said they were attacked by bandits." Joy knelt by the man on the floor, appalled at the whiteness of his face, so in contrast with the bronzed neck exposed by the open collar of his shirt. Rich red blood streaked it like

Indian war paint.

With steady fingers, Angus poured whiskey the length of the furrow, gently probed it, poured on more whiskey, and shook his head. "We need a doctor, but we canna both leave him and what of the other lad?"

Joy's quick mind examined the possibilities. "Take Jenny, load up the boy, and bring him back. I'll watch over the two of them while you go for a doctor."

"Aye. Bring me clean cloths for bandaging the wound. The doctor will need to do stitching but we must stop the bleeding."

A half-hour later, the older of the two strangers lay on Joy's blanketed cot in her tiny room. Angus returned with the lad and they got him onto Angus's cot. "Now, if they wake, tell them they've been hurt but are among friends. I canna say how long it will take to find the doctor and get him here. If they ask for water, give it sparingly."

Joy nodded, but had to keep from crying out that she'd go for the doctor. It would be useless. Never would Angus allow her to go unaccompanied into Virginia City at night, even to save a stranger's life. Feeling this couldn't be real, she set herself to tasks that would release her from the trance she felt surrounded her: scrubbing the bloodstains from the floor, washing her hands, making a pot of coffee, and cutting bread for supper when someone wanted it. The beans she had left cooking earlier would serve and she opened a tin of peaches, costly though they were.

A low moan roused her from her stupor. She rewashed

her hands, dried them on an old towel, and hesitantly stepped into her room after a glance at the lad to see he still slept.

To her horror, the tall stranger sat bolt upright, eyes glazed. "Carlos, watch out!" he yelled. A spasm shook his body and he fell back as one dead.

With a little cry, Joy ran to him and gazed at the matted dark hair and parchment face that yet betrayed manliness and strength. She knelt beside him and poured out her heart in prayer, then slowly rose and braced herself for the long wait until Angus and the doctor arrived.

seven

All thought of mining fled before the grim necessity in the little shack perched away from Virginia City. Joy would never remember without a shudder the hours before Angus came back with the doctor. The boy named Carlos slept but twice more the other one roused. It took all the strength in Joy's arms to press him back against the pillow.

"You have been hurt. You are with friends," she repeated again and again. Yet he thrashed restlessly until Angus's bandages shifted and she had it all to do over. She also told him, "Carlos is all right," and he relaxed a little until the next spasm came.

The overworked doctor shook his head over the blood loss, rolled up his sleeves, and went to work. "He needs care but can't be moved." He eyed the white-faced girl. "Are you a good nurse?"

"I don't know, but I can follow orders," Joy quietly said.

"Good." The doctor finished his neat stitching. "He needs rest, broth when he can take it, and a chance to recover from the loss of blood. Wound's good and clean and shouldn't infect. Now, for a look at the other one." He strode into the front room that combined Angus's bedroom, cooking area, and living space.

"Hmm. He's lost blood, too, but not so much as the other one. Better put in couple of stitches." He did so. "Same orders. Rest. Quiet. Food."

"And prayer," Joy added.

The doctor's shaggy brows almost met above his keen eyes. "That, too. I'll drop in soon. If you need me before then, holler."

"What's your charges?" Angus inquired.

Joy caught the doctor's quick glance around the room before he gruffly said, "I'll collect from the parties I doctored when they're able to pay."

Joy swallowed hard at the goodness in the frontier doctor's reply. "We thank you."

"You'll need a couple of extra cots, looks like," the doctor said. "The lad will wake before the day's out and you can put him into the other room. I don't want the older man moved. I reckon you can put up some kind of curtain so Miss McFarlane will have privacy."

"Of course." Angus nodded. "In the morning I'll bring Jenny down. But where can I get cots?"

A grim smile crossed the doctor's face. "I have a couple that aren't being used just now."

Not until he had gone did Joy realize those cots had in all probability held some of the newest residents of Boot Hill. She pushed aside the thought. Squeamishness had no right to interfere with the task ahead. The strangers thrust into their home needed all her attention.

All night both Joy and Angus kept vigil. Once he urged

her to roll up in a blanket on the floor but she would not. They alternated between Carlos and the quiet figure in the little bedroom who moaned and struggled until a deep sleep claimed him. Joy also took what she would need into the other room.

"Is he dying?" Joy asked when his breath stilled. Her heart caught.

"I canna say. He's in our Lord's hands."

Yet when morning came, their unexpected guests both lived. Carlos opened his eyes, wildly looked around, then focused his eyes on Joy, who held a cup of water to his lips. "Señor Brit?" Fear shone in his face and in the way his long fingers plucked at the blanket covering him, even while he drank.

"He is alive and resting, which is what you must do," Joy ordered. "We are friends."

Carlos drained the cup and wearily closed his eyes after a low, "Gracias." He slept until Angus returned with Jenny and the cots, roused when they moved him in next to his friend, and smiled before drifting back into sleep.

"He is dressed like a peon but I'll wager he is pure Castilian," Angus commented. "His hands are patrician; so is the lad's manner. Brit, he called the other. Sounds like he's from the Emerald Isle."

"He rolled the *r* in Carlos a bit," Joy said.

They rigged up a worn blanket across one end of the main room and set up Joy's cot behind it and Angus's in the cooking area. She put away her belongings as best she could and set meat to cooking for broth, but with a heavy heart. Would "Señor Brit" rouse enough to sip it, or to recognize his friend in the cot beside him? The strangers had woven themselves into her life. She couldn't bear it if one of them died.

Strange days followed. Carlos, with the resilience of youth, good nursing, and high spirits, quickly bounced back. He dogged Joy's footsteps and clung to Angus's assurance that "Señor Brit" would indeed live, in spite of the fever that burned and left the tall frame wasted and pale.

The boy proved invaluable in relieving the McFarlanes with Brit. He set his hand to everything from sponging the patient with the least amount of water possible to helping cook. He made friends with Jenny and whistled dolefully, sometimes bursting into snatches of song when Brit became conscious. Carlos also saw faith in action. Never a day ended without his host and hostess kneeling in prayer. The first time he opened his eyes wide, then closed them and respectfully bowed his head. After that, he murmured prayers of his own, perhaps the first ever said before others.

Carlos also spared them the burden of expense for the two guests. As soon as he could coherently speak, he had shown them the clever way he and Brit carried money in the lining of their coats, with the seams sewn flat.

"Before the *bandidos* found us, we discovered much gold," he told them in a whisper. His dark eyes and white teeth gleamed. "No one knows where it is but us. We were on our way to your Virginia City to get more supplies. A man gets hungry when looking for treasure!"

Joy disciplined a smile. Not for anything would she laugh at this earnest boy who combined early manhood and a frank childlike zest for life.

"We see your little house but Señor Brit says not to stop for we are in one big hurry. A little way down the hill— *bang, bang* goes rifles. I see Señor Brit stagger, but he cries, 'Carlos, go on!' I obey. *Bang, bang* comes again. I stagger, too, and fall from my horse—"

"Your horse!" Angus protested. "Lad, ye had no horse."

"Horses we have. Two." He held up two fingers. "The *bandidos* take Shamrock and King, our faithful horses. I know nothing until I hear someone say, 'Come out, you wretch.' It is the so beautiful señorita." He bowed from the waist.

"But how did Mr. O'Donnell get back to the cabin?" Joy burst out.

"Ah, he is brave. He would crawl through cholla cactus and its long thorns to help me and I, Carlos Montoya, would do the same."

Quick tears sprang to the girl's eyes at the loyalty and love in the simple words and at the thought of the badly wounded older man somehow dragging himself back to their doorstep. If he had not managed it, both travelers would undoubtedly have bled to death before being found. What a rare and unusual friendship they shared!

Voluble Carlos never tired of talking about his comrade. He acted out with wide gestures how they first met, the slipping saddle, the rescue. He modestly related the incident on the mountain and shrugged when he said, "Dios, the good God, He made my rope go <u>zing</u> over Shamrock's head."

Even discounting the hero worship that made Carlos exaggerate, Angus and Joy grasped the worth of their other patient. Her heart rejoiced when she discovered he was a Christian—and she wondered why it should matter so much. The tenderness she felt frightened her. Never before had she experienced such feelings, a tugging at her heart. Rich blushes mantled her face and she thought how Angus had told her that when the right laddie came, she would know it. Could Brit O'Donnell be that man? She fled from her thoughts, yet reveled in each new facet of the young man's sterling character as portrayed by Carlos.

Yet the strange happiness blended with regret. Many times Brit cried out the name Dolores. Carlos frankly told them his sister probably cared for Brit as much as was in her fickle nature to love any man, but, "That one blows with the wind which is Papa's smile," he announced. "She will marry the man Papa says. That is why Señor Brit came for riches, to win Dolores."

Joy cried out, "Won't she marry him if he doesn't find silver or gold?" She found the idea repulsive, yet appealing.

"*Quien sabe.* Who knows?" He shrugged in the way they had learned expressed far more than even his most dramatic words. "Papa wants to get back his other haciendas and without money and power, he cannot do this. There are many who come to call on Dolores but few who are wealthy enough for Papa—or her."

A week after the arrival of their guests, Carlos strutted around proclaiming himself as good as new except for stiffness in his left shoulder and a little soreness. The second week he restlessly sought diversions. Brit had begun to mend and needed less care. He had ordered Carlos to stop hovering and leave him in peace from his loving ministrations that threatened to spoil him for life.

Carlos just grinned but availed himself of his new freedom by promptly getting himself into trouble.

It started innocently enough. Joy needed notions and a few things poor Angus couldn't pick out for her at the store. One afternoon while he puttered around the place getting everything in top condition so he could resume mining soon, Joy said she would walk down to Virginia City.

"I will escort you," Carlos gallantly told her and watched her tuck the gray veil over hair and face. "Why do you cover your beauty? My sister Dolores wears a veil but not such a thick one. It covers but does not hide, as yours does."

"Dolores doesn't live in a mining camp, lad," Angus dryly put in.

"Si." He assumed a wise look and opened the door for Joy. But once away from the house his boyish grin spread and he told her, "Curious I am to see this place. We kept away from such villages on our way here." He ran ahead in sheer high spirits.

"You know, Carlos, I never had a brother, but if I could choose one, he would be just like you," she impulsively told him.

"Gracias. How old are you, señorita?"

She hesitated. If she told him sixteen, which could be true, his regard for her might change from brotherly to a new feeling she didn't share. "Angus says I might be seventeen or eighteen," she said carefully.

"Might be! Does your papa not know?" He spun in the narrow path and faced her.

"No one knows. He found me in the desert after a sandstorm." She quickly filled in the few details known about the odd happening.

"Then you are not Señor McFarlane's daughter."

"Never say that!" She indignantly placed hands on her hips. "Daddy Angus says that as long as our Lord permits, I will be his lass."

He dropped back to walk beside her when the path widened. "Do you never wonder who you really are?"

"I am a child of God," she said gently. "That is most important."

"Si, señorita." As if sensing her reluctance to speak more he changed the subject. "You belong in a garden, not in this desolate land." He waved to the clutter of buildings and shacks below. "Ah, but you would like the Montoya hacienda. One day, perhaps, you and your papa will honor us by coming to Monterey."

"What's it like?" Joy asked. They spent the rest of their walk talking about the blue Pacific, the bright flowers, and how glad Carlos was that Señor Brit had come.

With the inquisitiveness of a child, Carlos poked into everything in the mercantile but backed off when Joy walked toward the ladies' department. "I will wait for you outside," he told her and sauntered out into the street.

Five minutes later, a roar like a wounded bull sent Joy, the storekeeper, and everyone within hearing distance to the spot where the slim Spanish youth, still in his peon clothes but wearing the hauteur of royalty faced a be whiskered, dark-garbed trio standing beside their horses.

"What's going on out here?" a saloonkeeper bellowed.

Carlos drew himself up in outrage. "Señor, these men, these *bandidos*, they stole horses and shot Señor Brit O'Donnell and I, Carlos—"

Woman's intuition warned Joy her friend must not disclose his Castilian heritage. Peons were tolerated but Spanish aristocracy signaled wealth in the eyes of the greedy. "Carlos," she called breathlessly before he could add his last name. "What is it?" She ran to this side.

"Those are the horses stolen from us." He pointed to the

bay and black geldings that flanked a white mare.

"Say, what is this?" the biggest of the men blustered. "We bought those horses fair and square."

A weak and ineffectual looking sheriff pushed through the gathering crowd. "What's carryin' on here?" He eyed Carlos with obvious disfavor.

"They stole my horse and my friend's. Señor Brit lies wounded even now."

"That's right," a voice boomed and the doctor stepped forward. "What are you doing here, you young rascal?"

"I am Señorita McFarlane's escort." Carlos shot back proudly.

"Well, I'll be," the big man said. "Nervy little rooster, accusin' us of bein' horse thieves!" He loomed over Carlos. "Run home to your mama, little chicken."

"I do not move without our horses." Carlos planted his feet a little apart and crossed his arms.

"Why, I oughta—"

"Hold it right there!" The doctor stepped between the boy and the bully looking miner. "Do you have a bill of sale for the horses?"

"Naw. Bought them off a feller just goin' through. He needed a grubstake. Right, boys?"

His two cohorts nodded and spat tobacco juice into the dust of the street, barely missing Carlos's boots.

"Do you have proof the horses are your, Carlos?"

Quicker than a bolt of lightning, Carlos gave a clear, high whistle then called, "Shamrock! King!"

The bay, then the black whinnied, reared, jerked their reins from the slack grip of the two who had been holding them, and leaped toward Carlos. With loud whinnies, they nuzzled him and pawed at the ground with their forefeet.

"'Pears to me they know the boy," the storekeeper observed in the grim silence that followed.

"Aw, any horse might do that," the burly man protested.

"But any horse isn't either of these horses, señor." Carlos's eyes glittered with deadly intent. "Black King has a single spot of white on his back beneath the saddle. Shamrock wears a scar under his mane on the left side, from the horn of a bull that once caught him."

"Well, sheriff?" The doctor forced the issue on the hesitant law officer, whose pasty face reflected his loyalties. The sheriff slowly came forward and motioned for King's saddle to be uncinched. It slid to the ground, revealing the white spot.

"Now the bay," the doctor reminded the wooden sheriff. With a resentful glance, the man parted Shamrock's mane and fingered the scar Carlos had said would be there.

Suddenly, the temper of the crowd changed. It began as a low protest, then swelled into rage. Horse thieves were as popular in Virginia City as Rocky Mountain spotted fever—and even less welcome.

"String 'em up!" someone howled.

"Dirty thieves," another called.

Horror filled Joy. She tugged on Carlos's arm. "Stop them! They'll lynch these men. You must not have their deaths on your soul."

Carlos just looked at her from fathomless eyes, caught up in the mob's thirst for revenge.

"Brit would not let this terrible thing happen," Joy cried, clutching Carlos's arm until her fingers bit into the flesh.

Slowly, the anger left the rigid boy's face and body. He turned to the group of furious men. "I have proved who owns the horses. I cannot prove these men are the ones who tried to kill us." He swallowed convulsively and his Adam's apple rose and fell. "I did not see who shot me or my friend. Perhaps he did."

With a sudden grabbing at the slipping shreds of his authority, the sheriff stepped into the situation getting out of control. "You fellers better hightail it out of town right now. The peon's willing to let you go, I figger, since he got what's his and ain't sure his friend can prove attempted murder."

"Si." Carlos's mouth turned down at the word peon but he responded to Joy's warning pinch and said no more.

Angrily, the leader of the trio mounted the white mare and spurred her down the street with his henchmen running behind.

The relief that overwhelmed Joy unbuckled her knees. Only her hold on Carlos kept her from falling.

"Señorita, we should go home." He patted her hand.

She nodded speechlessly. The crowd dispersed but the doctor and storekeeper lingered long enough to warn, "Young fellar, look out for those three. Chances are, they'll get out of here while the getting's good. On the other hand, they're just mean enough to lay for you."

Joy shuddered and Carlos had to almost lift her to Shamrock's back. The bay curiously turned his head and looked at her then patiently stood while Carlos resaddled King and mounted. They rode out of town with Joy nervously glancing over her shoulder but no one pursued them.

Carlos stayed strangely quiet for about half the way home then he reined in and turned his liquid gaze toward the girl. "Señorita, it would only worry your papa and Señor Brit to know everything that happened, si?"

Joy had been thinking the same thing. "We can't lie and they'll know we got the horses back."

"Ah, leave it to me. I, Carlos Montoya, will tell the story."

She giggled in spite of her upset condition. "There's no doubt about that!" Yet even she couldn't know how skillfully Carlos would blend truth and omission. When they reached the shack, he slid from King's saddle, helped Joy down, and tied both horses to the corner post of the house. Then he burst inside with a wide smile.

"Señor Brit, Señor Angus, the horses. In town we see them. I whistle and call. They come to me, the good Shamrock and King. At first, some men think they are not mine but I show them the white spot on King's back, the scar Shamrock wears. The men believe me and here we are!"

Angus looked skeptical and Brit raised one eyebrow but the fact of the horses' being there without harm to Carlos and Joy verified the story. Yet every time Joy remembered that mob crying, "String 'em up!" she thanked God those three men still had their lives, even though they stole horses, shot at innocent people, and lied. What an awful thing if they had gone into eternity unforgiven and bearing their sins.

eight

Closer and closer the bonds of cramped living and shared food drew the McFarlanes and their visitors. A few days after the recovery of King and Shamrock, Brit suggested that Carlos lead Angus to the strike they had made. Irish blue eyes had measured the Scotsman and his daughter and found them trustworthy. In turn Angus confessed he had also found what might be a rich lode, but he didn't have the money to develop and mine it.

"I never thought I'd take a partner except my lass," he said simply and held out his hand. A poignant light turned his gray eyes to molten silver. "Laddie, if ye are willing, so am I."

"I am." Brit shook heartily.

"And I." Carlos laid one hand on the clasped fingers. "Señorita?"

"It's an answer to prayer," she softly said and crowned the three hands with one of her own. "We have needed someone to help us. God surely sent you."

"I'd just as soon He hadn't been for letting me get shot in the process," Brit said wryly and touched his still-tender scalp that would always bear a scar.

Carlos, the irrepressible, had the last word. "Señor Brit

will always know now where to part his black hair."

Joy choked at Brit's scowl that gave way to mirth and Angus's rare laugh completely chased off the solemnity of the moment.

By packing Jenny and riding the geldings, Carlos and Angus could make good time to the strikes. The only problem was the propriety of leaving Joyous and Brit alone. Virginia City tongues wagged at the slightest hint of scandal and all eyes turned toward "the redhead that sings like an angel, and look kinda like one, too."

Betsy Mills solved the problem. When Joy mentioned that Angus and Carlos wanted to do some prospecting, the good woman up and told Joy she'd be happy to come stay at the shack.

"The reverend's been itching to get out and see some of the folks in the other towns around," she said bluntly. "But he doesn't aim to leave me here for the spell he'd be gone. It will be a favor to me and we can 'nvite folks right up there for midweek prayer meeting." Two days later she arrived, perched on the nag's back and beaming with Christian charity.

"Now, Mr. O'Donnell, we'll do some changing around," she announced. "You can have Joy's nest and she and I'll move into her. . .the room you've been using."

A flush spread over his face and his eyes gladdened. "I've been for telling her that's how it should be but she hasn't been for listening."

Joy just smiled and followed Betsy's orders. A niggling

little thought disturbed her tranquillity. Of late, she had spent hours talking with Brit while Angus and Carlos busied themselves elsewhere. Would Mrs. Betsy's coming change all that? She hoped not. Brit O'Donnell had opened up a new world to the desert-raised girl. She had sat for hours listening to his stories about Ireland, coming across on the miserable ship *Promised Land*, the struggles in the city, and at last, the welcome purchase of the farm in Maine. Her breath caught at the descriptions that flowed from Brit's crossing the United States.

"I've only been here in the southwest and California," she said shyly. When he asked where she was born, she told again the miraculous story of Angus's finding her in the desert and how all these years they had never uncovered anything about where she came from.

They talked of other things: of God and His Son and of Brit's introduction to the Montoyas.

"I've never seen a woman like Dolores," Brit said and a pang Joy couldn't interpret crossed his features. His eyes in their smudgy thick lashes darkened with thought. "She's exquisite. White skin and hair and eyes blacker than midnight at sea on a stormy night." The poetry of the Irish ran through his description until Joyous could almost see the proud girl.

"Does she love our Lord?" Joy hadn't meant to ask. The words seemed to come without her help.

He side stepped the question. "Her family is very religious, but in a different way because of their heritage."

He laughed ruefully. "And she's been spoiled, raised in the hacienda. She's young, though. The years and a good husband should change her into a real woman." He sounded more hopeful than convinced.

Now Joy sighed. Surely there would be no more such confidences. She hadn't reckoned with Mrs. Betsy, however. Every afternoon the minister's wife said she just had to have a "wee nap"—she imitated Angus—and that the two should walk so Brit could regain his strength. Joy suspected her of matchmaking and told her outright that the tall Irishman planned to marry Carlos's sister once they struck it rich.

A disbelieving eyebrow shot up. "Oh? Then why isn't she here with him? Monterey's a far piece from Virginia City, I'm thinking."

Joy managed to leave the room before she gave away too much interest in the conversation.

One autumn afternoon when blue haze hid the bustling town below and gold leaves fell like treasure from heaven, Brit and Joy stopped to rest on a rock outcropping. Content just to be near the man she had learned to love second only to God and unwilling to consider the future, Joy gazed unseeingly at the distant mountains.

"Joyous, what do you want from life?"

His quiet question caught her unprepared. It took all the effort she could make to keep from crying out, "Love, a home with a tall, blue-eyed man who will love, protect, and father my children."

Brit, obviously unaware of the turmoil beneath the worn blue-and-white check bodice of her dress, continued, "It's such a strange life for a woman like you. Do you ever be for wanting jewels and fine houses?"

Hot tears blinded her. How could she answer without giving away the secret only God knew or could ever know—because of Dolores? She faltered, "I loved our little home in California. We had everything we needed there." *But not all I need now,* her heart reminded. *Then I knew not of a woman's love for a man in my life.* Desolation fell on her like a blanket. Even when she and Angus went back, the place could no longer be home. Her soul and understanding had become enlarged and broadened with its hidden love. She could never go back to the childish contentment the farm offered.

"I don't mean to be for prying, but why did Angus bring you here?" His widespread hands indicated the surroundings.

"I've never known. He isn't greedy. He cares for wealth only for the good it can do." A pucker of her brow drove away other thought. "We had used most of what we had found in the California streams and hills but the farm gave us our living all those years." She sighed and twisted her hands, subconsciously comparing them with the slim, white hands of the absent Dolores. Sturdy, like her body, and hardworking, they fell short of perfection, although she kept her nails cared for and rubbed tallow into her hands to prevent chapping.

Did he suspect how troublesome the thought was to her, she wondered when he softly said, "One day the man our Father wants you to love will come, Joyous. Perhaps when you least expect it, the way love came to me the moment Dolores Montoya pulled off her man's hat and I discovered her to be a girl, no, a woman."

To hide the fresh pain his words brought to her tender heart, Joyous jumped up from the rock. "We must be going or Mrs. Betsy will think we've fallen into a canyon or something." She kept her face averted from the almost holy look of worship in Brit's eyes when he spoke of the Spanish woman he planned to impress and marry. She also decided not to spend so much time with him. Each time she did, it became harder to submit to his well-planned future and his talk of Dolores.

"What does he think of me, God?" she whispered one sleepless night when autumn's cold warned that winter lurked in the nearby mountains and crept lower each day. "I know we are friends, but why did I have to meet Brit O'Donnell when his heart is already given away?"

The answer to her questions came as suddenly as Brit and Carlos had done weeks before. Mrs. Betsy fell ill before Angus and Carlos returned from their expedition, even before Reverend Mills finished his circuit that reached as far as shacks and caves housed souls who needed to hear the gospel. One afternoon she laughed and joked in her usual way; a few hours later she cried out, bringing Joyous out of deep sleep.

"Are you for being all right in there?" Brit's voice came clear, along with his knock on the crude door.

Joy snatched a dressing gown, hastily donned it, and threw open the door after a quick glance at Mrs. Betsy, whose pallid face glistened with sweat in the moonlit room. "I think she's awfully sick."

In one stride Brit reached the bedside, gazed down, then ordered, "Bring a light."

She obeyed, but her fingers trembled so that she almost dropped the old lamp and Brit had to light it.

"Mrs. Betsy, what is it?"

Her ashen face and shallow breathing showed pain. "My side." She pressed her hand low on her abdomen.

"Do you still have your appendix?" Brit demanded. He turned back the covers and gently pressed her hand.

She gasped and her face contorted but her sense of humor held. "Brit O'Donnell, I'll have you know I've kept all the parts the good Lord gave me!"

"I suspect you won't be for keeping that appendix," he told her grimly then swung toward Joy. "Bathe her face in cold water. Don't let her drink or eat anything." He marched out into the other room with Joy at his heels.

"Are you sure it's her appendix?" She clutched his sleeve.

Brit nodded. "I've seen them before—in Ireland and on the *Promised Land*. He scowled. "And us without a mount." He shrugged into his warm coat. "Thank God for the moon. I'll come back with the doctor as soon as I can." He walked out and banged the door behind him.

For the second time, Joy remained in the cabin where death hovered in the shadowy corners. She faithfully kept cold compresses on Mrs. Betsy's face and neck, hating the agony in her friend's eyes and passionately wishing she could do more. What seemed days later but was in reality a short time, the *clop clop* of horses' hooves sent her flying outside.

"How is she?" Brit flung out even before he dismounted from his borrowed horse.

"The same."

The doctor grunted, slid from his horse, grabbed his bag, and hurried into the shack. Joy noticed the tail of a night shirt stuffed into his trousers.

A few minutes later, he announced, "This appendix has to come out." He ignored Joy's quick breath, Brit's low mutter. "Boil water. Get out sheets and—" His staccato orders sent the two who loved Mrs. Betsy scurrying. The crude table in the cooking area became an operating table. Every lamp and candle in the shack combined to provide light. Yet the doctor gritted his teeth and barked commands between clenched lips. Brit staunchly stood by his side, assisting, while Joy kept boiling more water, warming blankets, and a dozen other things the doctor commanded. An hour later, Mrs. Betsy lay white, spent, and minus an appendix, snugly tucked back in her cot.

The doctor permitted himself a smile. "Nice little job of stitching I did there," he said dispassionately.

"Will she be all right?" Joy quavered, unstrung by the rapidity of the happenings.

"Unless infection sets in. She's strong and healthy and I reckon the Almighty knows how much Virginia City needs her and her preacher husband." The doctor's gruff voice didn't quite hide his concern. He gave succinct directions for her care and added, "I'll leave the extra horse here, just in case you need me."

Brit said the last thing Joy would have expected. "Doctor, is there. . .will there be talk about my being here with Miss Joy? I mean, now that Mrs. Betsy. . .," he floundered.

"Son, what's got into you?" the doctor snapped. "She's still here, isn't she? Besides, even folks around here are willing to make allowances in time of trouble."

Brit didn't give an inch. "I just don't want any kind of gossip going the rounds about a woman like Joyous." His eyes flashed and a fighting-Irish look came into his face. "I'll not be for saying what will happen, should there be a slur cast."

The doctor laughed, but in subdued tones. It made him seem more human and less an efficient machine. His eyes twinkled. "Son, should that happen, this old sawbones will be proud to put in his fists along with you." He collected his stained instruments, plopped them into a basin of steaming water Joy offered, and began to clean them.

Mrs. Betsy slowly healed and without infection but time and again she said, "Land's sakes, I must be getting old. I just feel so poorly, as if I'll never be able to do a lick of work again."

The doctor scolded and told her not to worry, she'd be up and chasing dirt in a few weeks. Reverend Mills disagreed. He had been thoroughly shaken when he came from his rounds and found his wife flat on her back.

One day he called Brit and Joy aside and told them, "When she's able to travel, I need to get Betsy away for a time. This is no place for her, even with all your good care. She needs better food and, pardon my saying it, a little more comfort than Virginia City affords."

"I understand." Brit nodded, then walked away with a thoughtful look.

A day or two later when the miners returned with the news that no one had found their claims, Brit called Carlos aside immediately. In a moment, the dusty, but undaunted youth bounded into the little room where the reverend sat next to Mrs. Betsy. "Everything is settled." His black eyes shone. "I, Carlos Montoya, offer you the hospitality of my hacienda. Ah, Señora Betsy, you will love the flowers and the warm air and the blue sea."

She turned her head away to hide slow tears that escaped and tattled of her continued weakness. "Thank you, Carlos, but we have no money, no way to get there."

He growled low in his throat and drew his slim self up. "Pesos are nothing and you are my guests." He raised his voice and drowned out their protest. "Señor Brit and I will arrange everything."

Hope crept into Mrs. Betsy's eyes and a longing that eloquently spoke of her beauty-starved soul. "Oh, is it possible?"

Her husband capitulated. "It is a gift from God, my dear. We must thank Him and the Montoyas."

Joy hadn't realized how easily money could accomplish the near impossible until she waved goodbye to her friends who rode off in a well-padded wagon toward Carson City. She knew they carried funds enough to purchase passage by stagecoach, or if necessary, hire a team and driver of their own, to carry them to the California coast!

"Now Señorita Joy will have to come to Monterey," Carlos reminded.

Angus remained strangely quiet through the bustle of getting the Millses off except to say, "Joyous, the lad is right. Ye will want to see Carlos's hacienda one day."

"As soon as we mine all the silver and pan all the gold you have found, we will go," she promised. Yet her keen eyes noticed how tired and gray Angus looked. A pang went through her. Why, he looked old. Not the kind of agelessness Angus had carried for years but a deepening of furrows. His formerly gray hair had turned nearly white. How could she not have seen? A small fear sidled into her heart and she added impulsively, "I wish we had gone with the Millses. What need have we of riches?"

"Señor Brit must find much wealth if he is to marry my

sister," Carlos reminded. He hunched his shoulders and looked at the sky. "I think the snow comes soon." He shivered.

"You miss California, don't you, Carlos?" Joy softly asked.

"Si." He gazed west and south, then shrugged again and reverted to his usual cheery self. "She goes nowhere, my hacienda. In the spring we will go home rich men." He doffed his sombrero in a low boy. "All in Monterey will say, 'See Señor Angus and Señor Brit, they own great mines. Ah, there is Señor Carlos, but who is the beautiful señorita with hair like a sunset?' Then I will say, 'These are my friends.'"

Brit interrupted before Carlos could continue his prediction. "What they should be for saying is, 'If it were not for Señorita Joyous and her good father, three lives would have been lost. Their nursing saved Brit O'Donnell, Carlos Montoya, and Mrs. Betsy Mills.'" Frank admiration shone in his face. "Seldom it is that such a beautiful face is matched by a gentle, giving spirit, truly gifts from our Father in heaven."

Joy's eyes stung. The weariness of hard work and worry threatened, leaving her unstrung. Yet she rejoiced. Some day her path and Brit's would part, perhaps never to cross again. Yet until the day she died she would remember his tribute. . .and cherish it against the loneliness that lay ahead, the ache of knowing in spite of his bedazzled state, the man she loved would taste bitter dregs in the marriage

cup he shared with Dolores Montoya, who awaited him—
and his wealth.

nine

Two vows Brit O'Donnell had made: First, to work at any honorable job until he could provide for his family. Second, to somehow earn enough to be in position to approach Don Carlos Montoya and ask for his daughter's hand in marriage.

By the summer of 1861, he had accomplished both— along with his loyal partners Angus and Joyous McFarlane and young Carlos Montoya, who represented his parents. The three men had insisted that Joy be considered a full partner, although the law recognized no such claim on the part of a woman.

"So much for the law." Carlos carelessly waved aside such trivialities in their meeting. "We will simply declare two parts of all we find to be Señor Angus's share and one for each of us." His amazingly simple solution met with instant approval from Brit and a little more reluctance on Angus's part.

Snow white hair topped his thin face and waved when he demurred, "Ye have put in more money toward developing and running our mines."

"Si, but there would be no mines and no Carlos or Señor Brit if you had not found and cared for us," Carlos flashed back indignantly.

They finally agreed. To Joy's surprise, Angus insisted that it all be drawn up legally and on paper. Until then, all transactions had been on trust.

" 'Tis to protect the remaining ones should the unexpected happen," Angus explained and the others nodded. They went to the finest and most honest lawyer they could find and came away with papers he said would stand up in any court in the newly declared Nevada Territory. President James Buchanan had signed the act in March. Two days later, the newly elected President Abraham Lincoln appointed a New York City politician, James Nye, as governor.

Before the territorial government could be set up in Carson City, southern troops fired on Fort Sumter, a Charleston, South Carolina military post, opening the door to the Civil War. Now tremendous importance of the Nevada gold and silver resources boosted production. Both North and South needed money to pay for the war. President Lincoln wanted those resources for the Union—which most Nevadans favored—and needed another state to bolster his antislavery amendments. However, Nevada Territory simply didn't have the more than 127,300 residents necessary to become a state.

"California is a free state," Carlos boasted. "Never will there be slaves in its great borders." The same longing that had softened his midnight eyes months before now returned, along with an almost imperceptible sigh that Brit caught.

Brit also sighed. Letters to Dolores were of course not permitted for they were not officially affianced and his only news of her came through infrequent epistles from the family to Carlos. He began to consider the future. He and the others had reaped the rewards of their work. They no longer lived in a shack but in a well-built two-story house big enough for them all. Why shouldn't they sell out, make a clean sweep, and leave Virginia City? His heart beat fast. He could keep his vows to his family and to Dolores. Two long years stretched between the time he and Carlos rode away from Monterey.

A great longing drove him to seek out Angus, who frequently commented he'd just rest a spell, now things were going so well. He found the old man sitting on the porch of the house that stood on the site where the shack had been. Laughter from the kitchen told him that Carlos and Joyous wrangled over some trifle and were safely out of the way.

"Angus, I'm for selling out our holdings and moving on."

The old prospector's eyes lit up. "Lad, it is glad I am to hear ye say it." He cocked his head and lowered his voice. His direct gray gaze peered deep into Brit's heart. "All these months, I've watched ye. Now I want to give ye the most precious thing I have."

Brit involuntarily started.

"Lad, my time is short. It's only been extended

because I asked our Father to let me live until I could find one worthy of a great trust."

Brit's throat choked off. "No, Angus. Why, if you're sick we'll get you the best doctors in Carson City, or in California—"

"Nay, lad. Listen while we have the time. I've thought it out in my mind and I don't want Joyous to know until the end is verra near." More and more a Scottish burr crept into his speech and his eyes gleamed with righteous zeal. "My last days are to be ones of happiness, as all the years I've had the lass have been. But when I'm gone she will need a man to help her. At one time I thought 'twould be Reverend Mills, but since he and Mrs. Betsy felt called to stay in California, it's not to be. Britton O'Donnell, will ye vow to care for my lass the way I have done, to see she isn't troubled by those who crave her fortune? What I have will be hers. Will ye do this for an auld prospector so he can meet his Maker knowing he did the best he could for the sweetest bit of womanhood ever to walk this Nevada Territory?"

"With all my heart, I will." Brit's strong hands shot out, caught the other's timeworn fingers, and held them. "Even though you may be for living a long time yet."

Again Angus shook his head but the somber look in his face had lifted and changed to relief. "Nay. The good doctor has warned me the Lord is counting down my days."

"Don't you think Joy has a right to know, so she can be

a bit prepared?" Brit demanded when their handclasp ended.

"P'rhaps. Yet knowing canna prepare her." Truth rang in the wise old Scotsman's voice, grown strong by Brit's vow. "Knowledge would make her suffer our parting not once, but a dozen times. I have your word ye won't tell her until I say?"

"You have." Brit felt his self-control leaving him. The months and years he had known Angus had deepened gratitude for his rescuer into love for him and for his adopted daughter. Not the kind of love that flamed in his breast for God or his love for the woman Dolores, but respect, caring, and appreciation of two persons who trod as best they could in the steps of the Master. The old prospector and the waif of the desert had woven invisible strings around Brit's heart, ones he knew would never be broken.

"Now, about the mines. Sell them for the best price. Sell the house here, too." Angus's rare smile made his craggy, worn face radiant. "Either I'll go with ye to Monterey or ye will take the lass. Should the girl ye love not welcome her, ye are to follow the instructions written in this wee packet." He took a folded bunch of papers, grimy, bearing mute witness of being carried around for a long time, from his shirt pocket. "This tells ye how to see Joyous to the home of the Millses. The deed to the little California farm is there, as well. Give it to Joy along with the letter. And lad, see to it she knows the greatest gift God ever bestowed on me was my finding her that day long ago." He rose and stepped off the porch when light footsteps warned them their tryst was about to end. "I'll just walk a bit so she canna guess. . ." He swallowed the words and went around the side of the house.

The woman who chased Carlos onto the porch was, at nineteen or twenty, just a little older version of the girl Brit first saw when he opened his eyes after the accident almost two years before. The same reddish gold hair. The same vivid blue eyes that could shadow or turn brilliant in the tanned face adorned with the ever present gilt freckles. Tall and strong, she could work all day and not tire, sing at the little church built by Reverend Mills's successor, and capture the hearts of Virginia City's finest.

Why hadn't she responded to one of her suitors, Brit wondered, amazed at the sense of loss the idea brought. All this time that Joyous had been their companion made the thought of another claiming her repellent. A new thought nagged at him. If what Angus predicted happened, then the man appointed as Joy's guardian must see her safely through the often stormy process of finding a husband! Brit wracked his brain. Why, not one man in Virginia City was worthy of her purity and innocence. Of course, once they reached Monterey, plenty of admirable, God fearing men would be available. Why then, did he shy away from the thought? Surely, he couldn't be so dog-in-the-mangerish as to resent the change in their friendship that a husband would bring.

"Carlos, if you insist on gobbling up my cookies, what can I serve to the ladies who come for tea?" Joy placed her hands on her hips. Her apron billowed out around her.

"Am I not more important than these ladies?" He raised his eyebrow and the girl's lips twitched.

"Aren't you ever going to grow up?" she asked.

"Señorita! I am eighteen and a man these many years." His outraged dignity suffered an eclipse when he added, "Most of my comrades have a wife and *muchachos* by the time they are eighteen."

"Heaven forbid." Joy threw her hands into the air, then a teasing glint came into her eyes. "Of course, I have noticed some of the girls watching you when we walk to the stores."

To Brit's amusement, Carlos for once appeared at a total loss for words. He turned deep red and, without a reply, spun on his boot heel and went back into the house.

"What was that about?" Brit asked the laughing Joy.

"He has an eye on one of the girls, Sadie, I think her name is. She's a nice little thing; her father just bought the mercantile."

"Sadie Bishop?" Brit remembered the pert face of a girl whose innocent eyes reminded him of Joy's; she had waited on him in the store. "I wonder what Don Carlos and his wife would say to their son and heir's attachment to a storekeeper's daughter?"

"Are they really so rigid?" Joy dropped to a rocking

chair.

"Impossibly so. Family means a great deal to them." Brit stared unseeingly down the hillside toward town. "I'm not sure they'll accept me, in spite of the fact we will return with enough to restore their lost property and more."

"Then they're fools." She flounced out of the chair and back inside before he could respond, but Brit saw anger deeper than he'd known she possessed in her sidewise glance when she passed him.

A little chill slid down his spine and words he'd overlooked in the emotional moments with Angus repeated in his brain. *Should the woman ye love not welcome her, ye are to follow the instructions. . . .*He shook his head impatiently. Of course Dolores and her family would welcome Joy, as warmly as they had opened their doors to the Millses, who stayed with them a few weeks before moving on. Why, as Carlos had said, if it weren't for the McFarlanes, neither of the California travelers would be alive. Yet once the seed sprouted, it grew like sunflowers. Suppose Joyous took a dislike to the Montoyas, despite her sisterly affection toward Carlos?

"Don't be daft," he ordered himself and firmly fixed his mind on considering the upcoming sales of house and mines, to the extent that he put aside at least temporarily all thought of possible conflict between Joyous McFarlane and Dolores Montoya, each beautiful in her own way, yet as different as midnight and noon.

All during the financial arrangements that would free the McFarlanes, Brit, and Carlos from Virginia City, Brit watched Angus carefully. His eyes told him what his heart chose not to believe. The old prospector failed a little each day. Did Joyous know? Sometimes Brit felt she must. A quick turn of her head or the faintest sparkle in her lashes when her gaze rested on her father shouted that she, too, recognized but could not admit how short Angus's time on earth would be.

Many times when the young woman and Carlos had gone out of earshot, Angus talked with Brit. "At first I honestly tried to find out who she was," he confided. "Then when all trails ended in the sand, I let it go. Now I canna say I did right by her, although it turned out well. She will never be in want and ye will see to it she's cared for."

Brit could only nod. A great void yawned in his life, the time when Angus would walk his final trail and part until they should meet again with their Father and His Son.

Another time Angus said, "There's a wee dress, the one Joyous wore when I found her. It's carefully packed. I've always thought it might lead to her own folks. Someday, when her heart lifts from the sadness of my passing, ask to see it."

"I will." Brit laid his hand on the other's frail shoulder. "You are not to be for worrying over Joyous. I'll guard her as you did."

"I know." The two words expressed a depth of confidence and trust beyond any Brit had ever known.

Of the four, Carlos seemed least aware of Angus's final battle. Seventeen-year-old Sadie Bishop's soft pale hair, smooth pink-and-white complexion, and shining blue eyes had enslaved him. The fact that her father despised him only added to the enchantment. "Her papa, he doesn't know I am a rich man," Carlos exulted. "Sadie does not know, either. She loves me, Carlos Montoya, for myself. Soon she will be eighteen. If her papa does not give his consent, I will steal Sadie and ride off to a padre, quick, before the papa can catch me."

"Don't do anything so stupid," Brit advised, then sighed at love's young dream shining in his friend's dark eyes. Who was he to tell Carlos what to do? If Don Carlos Montoya refused his suit and Dolores were willing, wouldn't he do the same?

In the space of a single week, everything changed. Brit sold the mine and the house to a rich speculator. Word leaked out and Carlos found himself welcome as desert flowers in the spring at the Bishop household. Sadie celebrated her eighteenth birthday with a small party and a perfect diamond solitaire on her fingers.

In the midst of rejoicing came a somber note. Angus could put off telling Joyous no longer. The ever-increasing tightness of his chest made it hard to breathe. He chose to break the news on a beautiful early autumn evening when all four of the family plus Sadie sat on the front porch and watched colored leaves whirl and softly settle in bright piles.

"Lass, all these years our Father has kept my wornout heart beating. But now it's weary. I am tired, too. I canna say how many days I will remain with ye, but they are sure to be few. I'd not have ye grieve too much or too long. Ye will be well cared for. Britton has given his word. There's nay to keep ye here and it's my wish ye go to Monterey with the others. I'm predicting Sadie will accompany ye." He paused and the pretty girl blushed.

"Ye are a rich woman, Joyous, but not just in gold and silver. Ye have the *Auld Book* for your guide, the love of our Father, and the eternal thankfulness of the old Scotsman who's been proud to have ye call him Daddy Angus.

"I'm not one for a lot of foolish talking, but when the time comes, Britton has a little packet for ye that will bring comfort."

Joy sat quietly. Only one tear escaped to show her sorrow. Brit had never admired anyone more. He thought of his own father, his mother, Katie, and the lads. If 'twere one of them, could he refrain from breaking down, even for their sake?

Angus wasn't quite finished. His tired, gray eyes looked toward the distant mountains above town. "I'd like for ye to put my bones to rest by the big rock over there." He pointed. "Brit has already asked the new owner and he has no objection. It's far enough away from the house not to be in the way and a cairn and marker can be fenced off."

"We'll do what you want, Daddy Angus." Joy left her chair and knelt by his side.

The old man rested his hand on her bright hair. "Aye, but it's a bonny lass ye are. I never told ye but once, choosing not to spoil ye. Always remember, our Father is with ye."

"Daddy. . . ," she hesitated, took a deep breath and went on, "are. . .are you afraid?"

The question hung in the silent evening air. Birds and squirrels had long since sought nests and trees. Carlos held Sadie's hand tightly, his dark eyes filled with compassion. Brit waited, unconsciously hoping for he didn't know what.

"Lassies and laddies, ye know how I've loved the desert and mountains, the canyons and valley. I've hankered to see beyond them all, over peaks and hills. Now I'm just wearying to know what's around this next corner."

Joy's eyes filled. So did Sadie's. Brit and Carlos gazed at each other in wordless brotherhood.

Angus looked at each in turn and brought his gaze back to his daughter's downcast head. "Ye all know I won't be riding the trail alone. Jesus has promised to be with us always and I ken that means going with me this time, as well."

The rim of the sun dropped below the horizon. A rosy flush bathed Virginia City and its surroundings with a heavenly light, tinging the faces turned toward it, and filling them with glory—a fitting end to a life well-lived.

Three days later, Angus started that last journey with a smile on his face and the radiant assurance of one who knows and loves his Lord.

ten

Early one bright fall morning, the four passengers who boarded the Carson City stage heading west attracted a great deal of attention from the loungers on the boardwalk. The tallest, tabacco-stained about the lips and wearing an air of importance, proceeded to inform the others in a half-mumble just who those passengers were.

"See the tall gent carrying the heavy case? That's O'Donnell, part owner of one of the biggest mines in the territory. Just sold out for more money than we'll ever see in our lifetimes! The Spanish one's a partner an' the light-headed gal in black is his wife. Purty, ain't she?" His bold gaze crossed Sadie from the crown of her bonnet to her sturdy shoes.

"Who's the gal wearin' a veil? Can't see much of her face but there's a hank of red hair."

The informer snorted. "You shore are dumb. That's old Angus McFarlane's orphan kid he found in the desert. He struck it rich and went pards with O'Donnell and the Spanish kid. The gal's a walking silver strike. Wish I coulda known her better. If I'd guessed what that old Scotsman—he's dead, now—was up to, I'da gone to meeting every Sunday. She's got the voice of an angel and even without being rich, that gal's worth getting religion for."

Mercifully, the quartet being discussed missed the lout's soliloquy. He escaped a drubbing by Brit or a challenge to a duel by Carlos, who considered their ladies joint responsibilities as well as wife and friend.

Joyous's name belied her heart when they settled inside the stagecoach. She did say, "I'm glad we're the only passengers" and Carlos winked at Sadie, while Brit hid a grin. She needn't know they'd bought up all the places in the coach to ensure a degree of comfort, much to the chagrin of disgruntled passengers who must wait and take the next coach west.

Angus and Joy's wanderings had led them mostly in the Utah-Arizona-Nevada-eastern California area, so once the travelers crossed the Sierra Nevada Range, she lost some of her sadness in sheer wonder. How different the terrain to her desert-accustomed eyes! She stared out at a new world and something stirred within her. Ever since she looked into the heavens to say her goodbyes to Angus, knowing only his frail body lay in the well-marked grave, dread of the future without him had gnawed like a mouse nibbles cheese. Seeing a new and splendid part of God's creation helped her accept the present, while still cherishing the past, although mourning the sale of Jenny.

It took them a long time to reach Monterey. Shamrock and King trotted along beside the coach, relishing patches of lush grass that appeared, cool lakes, and rushing streams.

"There are many horses on my hacienda," Carlos told his charming bride. "You may have any one except Sol." Longing crept into his face. "It will be good to ride that horse again, señora." Then he laughed when Sadie blushed, still unused to her new name but wholeheartedly in love with the dashing Carlos.

"Did you send word to your parents that we are coming? And that you are bringing a bride?" Brit sternly asked at a rest stop, making sure the women didn't hear him.

Carlos immediately put on a wounded look of innocence. "Si."

"Are yor sure?"

"Señor Brit, have I ever lied to you?" Carlos's eyes flashed.

"You certainly have a temper! I just want to be sure we're expected." Curiosity made him pursue the subject. "What did you say in your message?"

Carlos raised his eyebrow in the maddening, endearing way he did so often. "Coming home. Bringing bride. Brit O'Donnell and Carlos Montoya."

Aghast, Brit could only stare. "But. . .they will think I'm the one who's married," he protested. "What will Dolores do?"

Carlos leaped into the air and struck his breast with his arm. "A fool. That's what I am." He lost every semblance of his cheerful personality. "Señor, I am sorry. Dolores, she will be a madwoman, and I , Carlos Montoya, have done this thing! Si, it would be better had I never been born."

Brit managed to laugh through his presentiment that an icy reception awaited them. "Don't be for making it a tragedy. And do not tell Joyous or Sadie."

Carlos's white smile broke like a wave on a reef. "It will be a good joke on Dolores. First she will rave, then she will cry. Perhaps it will make her look into her heart." His eyes filled with dreams. "Who knows? If she should marry out of. . .what is it. . .pique? The so beautiful Señorita Joyous is worth many Doloreses, even though I love my sister dearly."

Angry at the young man and not knowing exactly why, Brit retorted, "Don't ever say such a thing again! I am Joyous McFarlane's guardian, nothing more." He added for good measure, "You insult both of us when you think differently."

Carlos hung his head, temporarily subdued.

Brit turned to see Joy vanishing into the stagecoach. His heart dropped like a cannonball. Had she heard, without understanding? *Dear God, don't let me hurt her in any way,* he fervently prayed, more upset than ever with the harebrained Carlos.

To his relief the young woman acted no differently on the remainder of the journey than she had before. A few times Brit caught a questioning look in her blue eyes but so fleetingly he couldn't be sure he'd really seen it. Other than that, the trip continued, day after day until one shining afternoon the weary travelers glimpsed the Pacific Ocean in all its sunset majesty.

Even Carlos, the eloquent, did not cheapen the moment by comparing the colors of sea and sky to Sadie's eyes and Joy's hair. He simply removed his sombrero, now stained from hard use. Tears welled into his eyes.

Brit experienced the same feeling of homecoming and vowed to send for his family as soon as he could find a home for them near Monterey, a farm whose rich soil would delight them, with flowers and shrubs to brighten their lives.

Sadie said nothing, just moved closer to her husband for comfort and protection in this new land. If her heart beat faster beneath her traveling dress, only she and God knew.

Joy left the others and wandered down to the water's edge. Tiny waves advanced and retreated, stained red and orange and rose from the dying sun, topped by lacy white froth. Seeking solitude, she walked along the shore, desperately wishing Angus could be here to share the moment, unselfishly glad he had gone from his pain-wracked body. "Father, I thank Thee," she whispered. "Be my guide."

Not until darkness dropped like a stage curtain at the end of the spectacular ocean show did she turn back to the others, grateful they had understood and respected her need to be alone.

That night, California stars hung low. Joy thought of the little farm miles south in a different part of the state, but without regret. She would continue to keep it even though she might never live there. It represented happy days, growing up memories. Sometime, she would go back, but not yet. Not while Angus's dear, dour face rose a dozen times a day to remind her of the past.

She turned her thoughts to the Millses. Brit had said they relocated in a tiny village not far from Monterey. Soon she would be able to see them again. A great rush of longing especially for Mrs. Betsy, with her round face and common sense assailed her. Joy fell asleep with the word *soon* singing through her mind, accompanied by the soothing *lap, lap* of the Pacific Ocean's tides.

Brit had pondered continuously about the best way to approach the Montoyas. If they simply showed up with Sadie and Joyous, surely unpleasantness and possibly hasty words would follow. He took Carlos aside, outlined a plan, and, with the rather subdued young man who must now present an unknown bride to his proud parents, approached the young women.

"Carlos sent a message that we were coming and bringing a bride, but I'm wondering if it might not be for the best to have us go ahead. You charming women will want to exchange your traveling outfits for something lighter and cleaner, I'll be thinking."

"Oh, yes!" Quiet Sadie gasped. Her cheeks pinkened.

"I. . .I want to wear the white gown I wore for my wedding."

"Si, the beautiful gown in which you became the señora of Carlos Montoya," Carlos quickly agreed. His eyes sparkled. "Mama and Papa, even the beautiful Dolores will say, 'Carlos, how could such a flower let one like you pluck her?' I will say, 'I think the good God must have made it happen.'"

"Joyous?" Brit turned to her, standing silent among them.

"I, too, wish to change into another gown." Her wan face smote Brit to the heart. While Sadie looked forward to entering the hacienda as its son's bride, Joy was dependent on whatever welcome the Montoyas offered. She seemed so alone, so troubled.

"My gown will not be white," she added. "But I purchased a dark one in Carson City. It isn't very nice but it's all I have."

"And you with a fortune," Brit teased.

Soft color stole to her hair. "I haven't become accustomed to having money to buy things," she confessed.

A little later the men of the party established their ladies in comfortable rooms in a well-known inn and strolled outside. Carlos grinned. "Like Señorita Joyous, I, too, wish to change." He fondly looked at his shabby clothes. "I will keep these garments to remind me how hard a man must work and how good God is. If we had not gone to Virginia City. . . ." He let his voice trail off.

Brit found himself silently echoing his friend's sentiments. He broke his reverie by clapping Carlos on the back. "Let's go find the best this town has to offer, for us and for Joyous."

"Si." Carlos's eyes glistened. "She must wear black and respect the memory of her father, but how gorgeous a black lace mantilla would be on her sunset hair."

They found it in a small shop, delicate as spider webs, glistening with dew, black as jet. "It is made by hand, señors," the eager merchant told them. "Very costly, though." He eyed his customers dubiously but became all smiles when Carlos magnificently pulled out a wealth of money. "Ah, but señor knows quality."

"Si." Carlos carelessly tossed him the price and Brit fingered the cobwebby mantilla. "She should like this."

"Señor!" The outraged proprietor fairly tore his hair. "I cut out my tongue, I throw myself into the sea, should your señorita not say this is the finest mantilla she has ever owned."

They left before the man could promise other bodily harm to himself and, when they got away, Carlos wickedly added, "Of course, this will be the finest; it is the first mantilla la señorita has owned. That gray stuff she hid behind in Virginia City is a rag compared with our gift."

Joyous found it hard to hold back tears when Carlos

triumphantly pulled the exquisite black mantilla from its brown paper wrapping and dangled it from a slim forefinger. Ever since she had unwittingly stumbled into hearing Brit's scorching rebuke to Carlos, something inside felt dead. "I am Joyous McFarlane's guardian, nothing more. You insult both of us when you think differently," Brit had said in a voice colder than the Sierra Nevadas in January. Not even a trace of friendship lightened the statement.

"What did you expect?" Joy flayed herself a dozen times. "You've always known Dolores is the only woman in the world Brit can see." Why then, did her sad heart long for the warm comradeship that seemed strangely missing on the latter part of their journey?

She raised her head after trying on the mantilla and saw and unreadable expression in Brit's eyes. Kindness? Surely. Guardians were usually kind to their wards, novels to the contrary. Admiration? Perhaps. He would want her to make a good impression on the Montoyas.

Joy gave up trying to identify what else flickered in his gaze and turned to Sadie, who clapped her hands and said, "It's perfect!" In her naive way she rushed on, "And so effective—you all in black and me in white." Pretty color came to her face when the others laughed but she soon joined in. Sadie might still be a child in many ways but she had already developed the womanly ability to laugh at herself.

Carlos stepped into the little pool of silence following

the merriment. "One hour from this time we will return for you," he solemnly promised, black eyes alive with anticipation and excitement.

"We will be ready." Joy removed the mantilla and smiled at the young man who had truly become the younger brother she never had. A wave of affection swept over her. Regardless of Brit, Carlos would always be her friend. The Millses were near and God walked daily with her. Still, she watched out the window of the inn, peering through lacy ironwork and hanging flowers of incredible reds and pinks and purples until the two went out of sight.

Before donning their new clothes, Brit and Carlos had carefully groomed King and Shamrock until they shone.

"Quite the dandies." Brit grinned at their reflections in the mirror of the room they had taken for a few hours. Carlos, resplendent in the black and silver he had put aside for so many months, was enough to turn any girl's head. Brit's eyes shone with fun. "You'll have to let your señoritas know you have a wife," he teased.

"Poof for the señoritas." He disposed of them with a snap of his fingers. "You are the one they will admire."

"Hmm." Brit adjusted the lapel of his new suit. He had steadfastly refused to purchase Carlos's type of clothing, but his tanned face contrasted nicely with the stark white shirt and dark suit. "Since when are colleens being for admiring a swallow when it flies with a peacock?"

Carlos didn't respond and Brit glanced at him. He

looked as young and frightened as the fateful day more than two years before when Sol's saddle slipped and the spiked fence threatened. "What is it, Carlos?"

"I. . .what are Papa and Mama going to say?" The young man who had faced danger and death now trembled at the thought of what lay ahead at the Montoya hacienda.

"What can they say? Sadie is charming and your wife." Brit grinned. "You are always quick-tongued. Why not take the offense and charge right in, maybe calling that we have come back rich?"

The sparkle came back to Carlos's mischievous face. "Si!" He fell silent, riding from the inn to the hacienda in deep plans, while Brit rode as one bewitched, longing yet dreading the reunion with Dolores.

By the time they reached their destination, all of Carlos's aplomb had returned. The Montoyas did not know just when the travelers would arrive and were just sitting down to dinner at the long, dark table. True to his promise, Carlos motioned aside the serving maids, cautioned them to silence with a finger over his lips and a dreadful scowl, then adjusted his face into a smile, threw open the great doors, and posed in the doorway.

"We are here, Mama, Papa, Dolores—and we bring riches enough to buy all the haciendas taken from us and many more!"

His bombshell had the desired effect. Don Carlos leaped from his place, eyes ashine. Although he had known the mines were doing well, he hadn't been told how well or the gigantic sum for which they sold. His dark eyes so like his son's gleamed. Brit could almost see the thoughts racing through his head, of a return to power as well as wealth.

Señora Inez did not move, but her face reflected her husband's reaction. Satisfaction fairly oozed from her still lovely features.

Only Dolores poured a drop of acid into the sweetness of their triumphant homecoming. Gowned in white, incredibly more beautiful even than she had been at eighteen, she rose with the mien of royalty, Spanish to the core. "So you have come back bearing gold and silver. Tell me, Señor O'Donnell, where is the bride you also found?" Her question slashed the air like a well-thrown knife. "Or is it that so soon she has deserted you, this woman you have made your señora?"

Brit couldn't decide whether thwarted love or wounded pride was uppermost in her disdain. Neither could he answer. Finding her here wearing white and a red rose had robbed him of speech as effectively as ruthless men stole other's gold.

"Well?" Dolores never once took her blazing gaze away from the man who loved her.

A peal of laughter shattered the growing tension. Secure in his welcome home because of the good financial news, Carlos seized his sister around the waist and swept her unbending body into a wild fandango. "Dolores,

Papa, Mama, it is not Señor Brit who brings the bride. It is I, Carlos Montoya, who has won the hand of the most beautiful señorita in the world except for my sister and Joyous, who share that honor."

Don Carlos dropped back into his chair, shocked.

His wife clasped her hands and turned pale.

Dolores wrenched free and stared at him with accusing, midnight eyes. "You! You? Why did you not tell me? she demanded. "We. . .I thought—" She turned toward Brit. "Señor, I have wronged you because of my wicked brother." She gathered her fluffy skirts about her and ran from the room. The sound of her sobs floated back to the frozen group near the table.

Brit took an impulsive step toward her, but Carlos intercepted him. "It is for me to go." He wheeled and followed in the direction Dolores had taken, leaving Brit to face the older Montoyas and their accusing eyes.

eleven

Just like Carlos, to vanish and leave him to explain, Brit thought resignedly. Excited voices speaking Spanish in the courtyard told him his young friend was having no easy time with his sister, however. The thought brought a cheerful smile to Brit's lips and hope to his heart. The change in Dolores's attitude in a twinkle of time spoke well for her feelings regarding a certain Irish suitor.

"Well, who is she, this señorita my son has married?" The same hauteur that marked Dolores's speech underscored every word in Don Carlos's question.

Brit weighed his words carefully, then told the Montoyas, "She is beautiful, charming, and young. She will give your son exquisite children. Her father has holdings in Virginia City and has recently purchased the largest mercantile there." He didn't add that Bishop also patronized the local saloons and radiated the good will sometimes generated by whiskey.

A feeling of relaxation ran from Don Carlos to Inez. "Why did you not bring her here with you?"

Brit didn't give an inch. Irish stubbornness could stand

up to Spanish arrogance. "Carlos didn't tell me the wording of his message to you until a few days ago. I realized then you could be misunderstanding the message. We agreed it best to come ahead and tell you the news, then return to the inn for the ladies."

"Ladies!" Inez lifted her patrician chin. "Does my son's wife have a chaperone?"

"No." Brit shook his head and silently prayed for guidance. "We are accompanied by a young woman, the daughter of our partner, Angus McFarlane, who died not long ago. He made me her guardian as she is young." He never once considered that Joy must be just slightly younger than Dolores.

The pupils of Inez's eyes dwindled to needle points. The welcome Brit had hoped would include Joy didn't materialize. "Señora Mills spoke of her, the waif from the desert. I must refuse her the hospitality of my home, señor."

"What?" Brit could feel his temper rise but checked it. "You don't understand. She is a wonderful girl, a Christian who—"

"Enough." Don Carlos didn't raise his voice but the tone warned that he agreed fully with his wife.

"It is not enough." Brit's eyes darkened and he faced them, ready to fight for the innocent girl-woman whose blue eyes shone with goodness. "When you know her you will see—"

"A girl who lived in a place with rough men, who

unveiled her face, and sang to *bandidos* and gamblers," Don Carlos said silkily. "Such a creature is not a fit companion for Dolores, or for one interested in our daughter," he added significantly.

He reminded Brit of a long, slim dagger, harmless in its case but highly dangerous when unsheathed.

"But. . .but she saved our lives," Brit protested. Were these proud Montoyas mad? "Both Carlos and I would have bled to death if she and her prospector father had not cared for us."

"Commendable. She shall be suitably rewarded." Don Carlos shrugged pious shoulders. "Such creatures can always use gold and silver."

The repetition of the word *creature* knocked the lid off Brit's boiling anger. "Joyous McFarlane is every much a lady as your daughter, sir." He folded his arms and tightened his lips into a grim line. "Whoever her real parents are, they must have been God-fearing and quality. As for Angus, who saved her life and raised her as his own, no finer man ever walked the West." A rush of emotion, gratitude, and love for the old Scotsman gave him courage to continue. "If Betsy Mills told you about Joyous, she must have told you the men of Virginia City looked on her as they do the angels."

Don Carlos lifted a peaked eyebrow and looked bored. Inez retreated behind her fan, as if this guest's ravings transgressed all the laws of good taste.

Sensing the hopelessness of continuing the argument,

Brit longed to hurl in their smug faces that if Joyous were not welcome at the Montoya hacienda then neither would he remain. The entrance of Carlos, bright-eyed and eager stilled the words but the keen young man could not help feeling the tension in the room.

"Don't blame Señor Brit," he pleaded, with a furtive glance over his shoulder at the now silent courtyard. "Only Dios could have kept me from my Sadie. When He did not. . . ." His satisfied smile and slight hunching of his shoulders finished the sentence. His smile vanished when his parents did not respond. "What is it?"

"Your parents have made it clear that Joyous is not welcome here." Brit couldn't have kept the bitterness from his voice if his love depended on it, which it did.

"Papa, Mama, what are you saying?" Carlos stared aghast, every trace of happiness erased from his white face. "Señorita Joyous, she is an angel. She—"

"Enough!" This time Don Carlos bland mask slipped and he actually roared. "Your own sister has suffered much on account of this woman. Ever since Señora Mills praised her, Dolores has borne an aching heart." Venom turned his words to a hiss. "When the message came, Dolores grew ill with worry that her brother and her *friend*," he stressed the word, "that they should be in the company of a nameless, homeless one dependent on the charity of a prospector, a common peon who—"

"You shall not speak of him that way!" Carlos cut into his father's diatribe. "Nor of Señorita Joyous. She is pure and good. She saved my life."

"So we have been told."

"And you still refuse to meet her, to lead her into the hacienda, bowing and burning candles because I, Carlos, do not lie dead?" Incredulity and disillusionment mingled with disbelief. "Without her, there would be no restoring of haciendas, no gold or silver or jewels and new gowns for Mama and Dolores."

"I have said she shall be rewarded." Don Carlos tapped the polished table, so shiny it reflected his fingers.

Carlos held his father's gaze for a single moment then with a disgusted snort turned on his shiny boot heel and strode toward the door. Brit followed.

"Where are you going? Why do you so rudely leave our presence?" Don Carlos's face turned purple and he shoved back his chair and beat the two men to the doorway. "Is it not enough that you came here with news of a wife?"

"And of gold and possessions," Carlos reminded with a curl of his fine lips. "At least Dolores is happy enough it is I who have a señora, and not Señor Brit." He brushed past his father and out the door with Brit right behind him.

"We will expect you and you and your bride to return immediately," Don Carlos called after the stiff, retreating figures. When they didn't look back or answer, he added with obvious reluctance, "And you Señor O'Donnell."

Carlos stopped and turned. "The day you welcome

Señorita McFarlane will be the day I, Carlos, return with my bride."

Such a heavy front door as that on the Montoya mansion couldn't slam but it did close with a dull thud that hardened Carlos's features and chiseled Brit's lips of stone. They mounted their faithful horses and rode back toward the inn. Not until they had stabled King and Shamrock did Carlos ask in a desolate voice, "What will we say to my Sadie and Señorita Joyous?"

"I don't know. I wish my family were here. We would all be welcome in their home."

Carlos visibly flinched and his face blanched. "She must never know what happened this night." His flat and lifeless voice hurt Brit and he blindly reached out a hand to the man who had cared for him for the past two years. "I can never forgive them, even though they are what they are."

Brit said nothing. This was no time to preach about honoring parents and the need to forgive, not when his hotheaded friend had been attacked by family tradition and narrow-mindedness. "It's been a lot longer than an hour since we left the inn," he mused. "Carlos, can't you think of anything we can say that will keep the truth from Joyous and yet not be false?"

Carlos despondently shook his head but a few minutes later he muttered, "I have an idea, but you must help me." In a few quick sentences he outlined his plan. Faulty though it was, Brit had no better suggestion.

"Carlos, you'd better be for acting like you've never done before," he warned when they knocked on the door and Sadie threw it open. A pang went through him. Radiant in her white bridal finery, Sadie's face looked pinched, her eyes haunted. Behind her, Joy's reddish gold hair gleamed against the black of the mantilla but every gilt freckle stood out on her pale face.

Carlos didn't wait for questions but tossed his heavily trimmed sombrero to a chair and encircled Sadie with his arms. Brit marveled at the way he smiled even while misery peeked from his eyes. "Oh, but Mama and Papa were angry!" He laughed and the sound grated on Brit's ears but drew an answering smile from Sadie and Joy.

"The heir and son of the Montoyas has chosen his own bride," Carlos announced dramatically. He released Sadie and smote his breast. "Such a thing always causes anger in Spanish papas and mamas. Always they fume and sizzle and when all is forgiven, they beam and say, 'Ah, our son has chosen well.'" He rolled his eyes and laughed again. "It is better not to visit them until this happens, si? Señor Brit and I have a so smart idea. We will take a little trip and see the good Reverend Mills and Señora Betsy until this storm from the ocean blows away and becomes desert sand."

Brit anxiously watched Joy to see if she could read anything more into Carlos's tale than what lay on the surface. Not a wrinkle marred her white forehead. Praise be. Anger at the insufferable Montoyas rose again and a

new thought. Did Dolores agree? Would she also revile
Joy? He wished for an instant he had never come back
and seen how truly beautiful the Spanish woman had
become. Once, they had faced the need for wealth. Now,
if he kept his third vow and carried the mantle of
responsibility that Angus McFarlane had bestowed on
him, it would mean the loss of Dolores forever. *If she is
all you believe and want, she will not let you go,* a voice
inside whispered. *If not.* . . . Brit refused to consider it.

Long after the men had said good night, with Carlos
graciously insisting that Sadie remain with Joy so she
wouldn't be afraid in a strange place, the orphan of the
desert lay wide-eyed. Something about Carlos's perfor-
mance had not been true. Why should the Montoyas
object so strenuously to their son's marriage? Yet what
else could have driven him and Brit back long after the
appointed time with the news they would not go to the
hacienda? Brit and his riches most certainly would be
welcome. That left. . .her. Insight flooded her mind.
Carlos's family must have refused to meet her.

Joy stifled a sob. She had no time to waste in crying.
After everything Brit O'Donnell had done for her and her
father, she must not stand in the way of his happiness,
even if Dolores were as selfish and vain as her brother
claimed and unworthy of Brit's devotion. Hour after
hour she lay planning. Where could she go? Not to the
Millses'. It would be the first place they would look if she
disappeared. If only it hadn't been necessary to sell

Jenny! But, there were other Jennies.

What if she crept from the inn at daybreak, hid herself until time to seek a burro, then rode south, back to the little farm?

She mentally surveyed her resources, pleased that a goodly sum of money lay stashed in the hem of her petticoat. For a long time she wrestled with the knotty problems. At last, she decided. Running away meant giving up her share of the profits from the mines and the Virginia City house, other than what she carried. She dared not let her friends know her destination or they would never consent to her going. Besides. . .her mouth twisted. Brit would need all he could gather to win Dolores Montoya. In a twisted way, her relinquishing her legacy would help him.

"Is this right?" she whispered, so low Sadie didn't even stir. "Father, go with me, I pray. If it be wrong, let them discover and stop me."

For the rest of the dark night hours, Joy lay planning her escape. Her heart ached, especially when she realized she could not take the trunks that housed pitiful mementos of her childhood. Only the clothes she wore would go with her. She considered the dangers of a woman traveling alone and remembered how she hadn't been able to bear parting with Angus's clothes. A warm jacket, pants, and shirt lay in the trunk. With her hair stuffed into his old hat, the heavy gray veil wrapped around her throat, she could pass for a boy. People would pay little attention to a boy on a burro, idly poking along.

Joy's heart pounded until it threatened to choke her when at first light she groped in her trunk, selected what she would need for her long ride to southern California, and donned Angus's clothes. She hastily ripped the stitches from her petticoat, hid her money inside her shirt, and stepped from the room, after a glance at Sadie, whom she had grown to love. Would she ever see her again? Her gaze turned to the battered old trunk. Surely, they would see that it got to the Millses'. Someday, when Brit had married Dolores and she could face the pain, she would come back and get her small treasures.

She had read stories of girls and women running away and secretly considered them improbable. Yet her own escape went more smoothly than she could believe. Joyous found a sheltered nook where she could wait and be away from the early morning chill, the corner of a deserted patio screened by flowers. Not until the sun climbed high and warmed the earth did she leave her haven, set boldly forth, and seek to buy a burro. She had wisely kept enough money out that by haggling with the owner through shaking her head vehemently and shrugging her shoulders she paid a surprisingly low price and rode away on her new Jenny. She stopped a few other places, purchased supplies here and there including a canteen, then turned Jenny east. Later, she would go south. A thrill of achievement lifted her spirits. The spectacular autumn day promised adventure, perhaps excitement, and she rode feeling she had done the right thing. It dulled the pain of parting to a low throb and gave her courage to lift her chin up and look ahead, not back.

Consternation remained behind the runaway. Brit and Carlos arrived at the inn after spending most of the night talking about the future. "We can't just be for imposing on the Millses," the older man said. "Unless we up and buy them a house big enough for us all!"

Carlos fitted the tips of his fingers together and showed a shrewdness much like his father's. "We will visit for a time, then—I know!" He leaped into the air, face lighted. "We will go to my Uncle Ramon and Señora Mary. They will rejoice and make the fiesta."

"Are you sure?" Brit thought of the quiet man and sad-faced woman he had met so long ago at the Montoyas.

"Si." Carlos sounded sure. "You wait and see. Now, Señor Brit, let us hasten to my Sadie and Señorita Joyous." He paused. "About Dolores. What will you do?"

"Nothing now." Brit's lips firmed. His Irish blue eyes looked more gray than usual. "Are you ready?"

"Si." Carlos snatched his hat and bounded out the door of their room. He chattered all the way to "his Sadie" but when she opened the door to his knock his mouth dropped open. Hair disarranged, eyes swollen and red from weeping, she flew into her husband's arms.

"She is gone. Joyous," she cried.

"What?" Brit stood petrified, staring about the room.

"It is true," the weeping girl managed to say. "See, her things are strewn." She pointed to the open trunk that bore mute witness of Joy's flight.

"Don't cry," Carlos softly said. "She cannot have gone far. Why did she leave? When?"

"I don't know." Sadie shook her fair head and misery filled the soft blue eyes. "I fell asleep with her here and when I awakened she was gone."

Carlos and Brit exchanged a steady glance before they crossed to the trunk. "Perhaps this will tell us something," Brit said. He awkwardly laid garments and a few books in neat piles outside the trunk, thinking how little she had, although Joy owned wealth. In the bottom of the trunk lay a small package covered by faded brown wrapping paper. He hesitated. What right did he have to uncover her possessions? He set his jaw. The right of a guardian worried sick over his ward outweighed other considerations.

"What is it?" Carlos crowded close with his arm still around Sadie, who clung to him.

Brit fumbled with the knotted string, then jerked and it fell apart. He pushed back the wrapping paper, reached for its contents, and held up a small, white dress. Torn lace hung from it like floating cobwebs. "Why..." Brit peered at the lace. A thrill went through him. "The lace. Carlos, I have seen lace like this somewhere!" He wrinkled his forehead and tried to remember but it eluded him.

"Lace is lace, is it not?" Carlos asked dubiously.

"You don't understand." Brit fingered the delicate stuff. "In Ireland we learned to know whose lace it was by the slight differences in the workmanship. Each lacemaker has a distinct style." He frowned again, feeling he held the key to not only Joy's whereabouts but much more in his hands. Why must knowledge elude him as a dancing butterfly?

Carlos took the garment from him, almost reverently. "It is old. It must be the dress Señorita Joyous wore when Señor Angus found her in the desert." He touched the lace. His eyes bulged. "But why would a lost waif wear a gown trimmed with real Spanish lace?"

"*Spanish lace*?" Brit snatched the garment back and held it close. "That's it. Carlos, this lace is identical to what bordered the handkerchief Dolores carried at dinner on the night I came to your hacienda."

twelve

Carlos stared at Brit as if he had gone mad. His eyes resembled pieces of obsidian resting on a white shore. He tore his gaze free and examined the lace again. "It is impossible," he burst out. "Do you not remember? Papa told you how Mama and Dolores have continued the art of lacemaking. Never do they sell or give it away except to members of the Montoya family—" He broke off. Color drained from his face, leaving it shocked and disbelieving.

"What is it?" Sadie cried. She tightened her grip on his trembling arm, eyes wide with alarm.

"Dios!" A prayer, not a curse. "Can it be?"

Brit wanted to shake him until he rattled. "What is it?" he hoarsely demanded, and clutched the time-yellowed child's dress.

Carlos took a deep, quivering breath. His aristocratic nostrils dilated. "Uncle Ramon and Señora Mary, the tragedy," he incoherently tried to explain.

"Carlos, get hold of yourself and tell us," Brit commanded. He vaguely remembered Carlos starting to tell him something about a tragedy long before that nearly drove Don Carlos's brother and his wife crazy with grief.

161

What had it to do with Joyous?

With a mighty effort, Carlos controlled himself. "They had but one child. One night she disappeared, stolen from her bed." He paused, licked dry lips, and went on. "From that night until this moment no one ever found trace of the child, although my uncle spent hundreds of pesos." He stopped for breath.

"You mean Joyous is that child?" Brit's head reeled. "Your cousin. . .and Dolores'?"

"Who knows?" A little color came back to Carlos's face. "We must go to the hacienda immediately."

"Wait, Carlos." Brit restrained his eager friend. "Before we do such a thing we must plan. What if it isn't true? We would be getting your aunt and uncle's hope up for nothing."

"Si, and perhaps they could not stand it." Carlos halted in his impetuous rush toward the door.

"Tell us more about the child," Saddie begged. Her eyes looked like wide blue lakes in her sweet face. "Why would anyone steal a child?"

"Everyone always thought it was a peon that Ramon had beaten for being lazy," Carlos slowly said. "He disappeared the same night as the little one."

"What was her name? How old was she?"

Carlos vainly sought to remember but shook his head. "The story is old and talked of only by servants. It happened before I was born. I don't know anything more, but Papa and Mama will."

All rancor over their heated argument the night before vanished before the monumental happening that lay ahead. Brit laid aside his personal feelings and agreed that all three would go to the Montoya hacienda. Don Carlos and Inez could tell them what they wished to know. If nothing came of it, Ramon and Mary need never know.

"Papa will never forgive himself if he has refused welcome to his own blood," Carlos said sadly. Compassion shone in his eyes. "Oh, if we had already known."

"Hold on. We still aren't for being sure," Brit reminded as they waited in the hall for Sadie to wash her face and tidy her hair. No bridal white with which to impress the Montoyas. Just a simple gray gown that enhanced rather than detracted from her lovely face now alight with hope for her friend.

Except for the change in clothing from evening dress to morning clothes, the large dining room at the hacienda matched the scene from the night before. Now the addition of Sadie bolstered Carlos. Again he made a dramatic entrance and announced, "We are here. I, Carlos Montoya, my Señora Sadie, and my friend, Señor Brit."

Dolores flung at him, "I thought you vowed not to return until we welcomed Señorita McFarlane."

Had she always worn that unpleasant twist to her

carved lips, that cruel look in her eyes, Brit had time to wonder before Carlos retorted, "Before many minutes pass you will regret your words and that you did not open your heart to her."

Dolores raised her chin an inch higher but subsided.

"Papa, Mama," Carlos turned to them. "What was the name of the child stolen form Uncle Ramon and Señora Mary? How old was she?"

They looked dumbfounded but Inez said haughtily, "It is long ago and not to be discussed."

"Pardon me, Mama, but it must." Carlos's face whitened. "It is possible we have news of the child."

"After all these years?" Dolores's peal of scornful laughter added nothing to her charms, at least in Brit's slowly opening eyes.

"Be still, Dolores," Carlos thundered. "Tell me, Papa. *What was the child's name*?"

Don Carlos sat even straighter and more rigid at the urgency in his son's voice. "Jessica. A most unsuitable name for a Castilian but Mary insisted on it. It means wealthy."

Quiet Sadie could contain herself no longer. "It is she," she squealed. "Jessica. Joyous. Don't you see?"

"What is this nonsense?" Don Carlos rose from the table, a forbidding look in his eyes.

Brit stepped forward until he faced the frowning man. He held out the little dress. "I saw lace like this on Dolores's handkerchief. Carlos says it is only made by her and her mother."

The elder Montoya's face turned the color of dirty wax but Inez stunned them all by rising to race around the table and grab the dress, so unlike her ladylike self that the others gasped.

"Where did you get this? I, myself made this dress for Jessica. She wore it first on the day she was five. When I bid her good night she smiled and said, 'My gown is beautiful. See, Mama hung it on my bedpost so I could see it when I wake.'" Tears streamed and her haughty expression crumbled. "That night she vanished."

"The date," Brit asked. "What was the date?"

"The fifth day of May, in the year of our Lord 1848."

Cautious hope flared in Brit's heart. "It fits. Angus McFarlane said he got word of the strike at Sutter's Mill several months after it happened on January twenty-fourth. He hadn't been near a village in a long time. He headed north and west."

"But how could the child be so far from home?" Carlos burst out.

"I don't know. Neither did Angus. Wait!" His fingers crept to his breast pocket where he always carried the small packet Angus had given him along with the letter to Joyous. Brit hadn't felt the time to be right for him to pass it on. Now, he brought it out and looked at it with troubled eyes. "I hope it is all right to open this." He scanned the circle of eager faces. Even Dolores had dropped her animosity.

"She would want you to open it," Sadie said, with a woman's insight.

Brit slipped his hand into the waterproofed covering, left the letter inside, and took out a single page. It contained a faithful retelling of the prospector's most precious desert find. Brit read it aloud. When he finished, silence fell.

"It would do no good to go to the place of burial," Don Carlos said. "Not after these many years."

"Then how will we ever know for sure?"

One by one they discussed their bits of evidence: Joyous McFarlane had been the right age at the time Angus discovered her. The dress, unless it were stolen, offered the strongest clue to the mystery. A child who referred to herself as J-yes might be shortening Jessica to Jess, as her mother somethimes called her.

"Also, she has blue, blue eyes and Señora Mary's eyes are blue," Carlos put in. "Although faded from sadness."

Brit spoke directly to Señora Inez. "What color is your sister-in-law's hair?" His fingers tightened into fists.

"Snow white, these many years. Once it was gold. When the sun shone, it made it glow like fire."

"Joyous has what Carlos calls sunset hair," Brit told them.

"Then we must hasten and tell my brother," Don Carlos shouted. His face twisted horribly. "To think that I turned her from my door, the daughter of my own brother!" His pride lay in ruins. "Bring her here this instant, the lost Jessica, that I might kneel and kiss the hem of her gown and plead for pardon!"

The light that had grown in Brit's heart at his friend's good fortune and the joy she would know from being restored to her real parents flickered out. "We do not know where she is," he confessed.

"What?" For a moment it appeared that Don Carlos would strike him.

"Papa, she went away. That is why we opened her trunk and found the little gown," Carlos explained.

His father sank heavily into his chair. His fingers twitched. "What can I tell my poor Ramon?"

"Say nothing until we find Joyous," Brit advised. "It would be cruel for them to know their daughter is found but lost again. We will do everything possible to track her down."

Don Carlos staggered up, leaned heavily on his wife's shoulder, and said to Sadie, "Little one, you are welcome here. Forgive our poor greetings. I. . .I must go to the chapel and pray that my sins be taken away." Then slowly he went out.

Carlos shrugged. "Almost, I feel sorry for him. But come, my Sadie. I must show you the hacienda." He sauntered off with a smile for Brit.

The large room felt too spacious for only two persons. Dolores suggested, "Señor Brit, would you wish to walk with me in the courtyard?" Her dimples showed in a daring smile. "We will be without a chaperone."

Brit nodded, thoughts still on the runaway. He absent-ly noted the heavy perfume of late blooming flowers yet it brought no heady feeling the way it had done two years before. Dolores led him to the same sheltered spot where he had kissed her and declared his love. How long age it seemed! Then, her little pout had charmed him. Now, he found himself annoyed at her coquetting in the midst of the earth-shaking events that had occurred.

"You do not listen to me," she accused. "Do you not love me anymore?" She measured her slight height against his own and looked up with mysterious, dark eyes.

He didn't answer.

She pettishly stepped away. "I wish you had never heard of this woman with the ridiculous name. Joyous. Joyous," she mocked. Angry flags waved in her white skin. "All you talk of is her. What of me, Dolores Montoya? Do you think I will always listen to your babble about this imposter? My cousin Jessica is dead."

Brit stood silently, arms crossed, gaze steady.

She caught her lower lip between white teeth and hissed, "Perhaps it is that you love her, not me."

He started to laugh. Stopped. A bolt from heaven could not have shaken him as much as the view into his own heart that came with her vindictive accusation. All these months while his memory of the Castilian he had put on a pedestal stood before him, had he been leaning toward Joyous, no, Jessica? Her steadfast eyes and

innocent face seemed to rise in the air before him and
cloud Dolores's darkening countenance. When it vanished, he felt a veil had lifted, the way Joyous threw aside
her veil when she sang the songs of salvation to those who
most needed to hear them.

With Dolores, he had idolized and had built in the
image of what he wanted his companion and wife to be.
In Joyous, everything any man could desire for a lifetime
resided in her sturdy body and healthy mind.

"Well, do you love her?" Obviously sure of an
impassioned denial, Dolores preened and allowed herself a small smile of triumph, her highest card in a
winning hand that never failed to subjugate her slaves.

"Perhaps." He wanted to shout and sing. He breathed
in the fragrance of flowers and of love. Before she could
reply, he bowed. "We have both changed, señorita. I
thank you for your hospitality." He moved toward the
door into the house feeling as if he'd been hit by a mule
and wondering how he could have been so blind.

A low gasp warned him. He turned. Dolores stood
where he had left her. Hatred shot from her eyes like a
tangible thing. Strong though he was, Brit quaked. He
had made an enemy for life. Yet her aristocratic upbringing considered defeat impossible. She turned her head
slightly, gave him a condescending smile, and said, "It is
well you have found someone to...console you. Papa has
arranged for a man of great wealth, far more than you and
Carlos found, to have my hand in marriage. The wedding

will be very soon now."

He had to admire her resourcefulness, although he'd wager said wealthy suitor had yet to learn of his successful bid. "I wish you happiness with all my heart," he told her and meant every word of it. How could a man not want everyone else to have joy—when that man intended to find his own Joy and spend the rest of his life, if necessary, convincing her she was the woman God meant to complete his days?

Sadie longed to go with Brit and Carlos in their search for Joy but her young husband overruled her. "We can go swift like the arrow on Sol and Shamrock," he said. "We find Señorita Joy in a little minute. Then we return and never again will I leave you." He bent low and whispered, "You can bring cheer to Papa and Mama, who are so sad."

"Dolores does not like me," Sadie told him.

"Dolores like Dolores." Carlos smiled in the way that usually got for him what he wanted. Sadie finally reluctantly agreed to remain at the Montoya hacienda.

"First we go to the Millses," Carlos declared.

"She won't go there," Brit disagreed. "Joy knows it's the first place we will be for looking."

"Of course." Carlos's eyebrows shot skyward. "But Señora Betsy will know the name of the little village where Señor Angus and his daughter lived."

"Wisha, wisha, but you're for getting wise," Brit said admiringly.

Naturally Carlos preened, but Brit insisted that before leaving Monterey, they first approach stage lines and owners of private conveyances for hire. The disheartening answer proved to always be the same. No señorita with eyes like the sea and hair like the sunset had boarded a stage south, or any other direction. No woman in black with a veiled face had been seen. Brit began to suspect Joyous had remained in Monterey but a thorough and quiet investigation of each inn and boarding place disclosed nothing.

A full week after reaching the hacienda, Brit threw his hands into the air and gave up. "If she's hiding here it must be in a crack in the adobe," he admitted. "Let's go see the Millses."

It didn't take long to reach the humble but pleasant cottage the Millses had found close to a tiny hamlet, little more than a crossroads, where the reverend preached and Mrs. Betsy mothered everyone in the small congregation. After the first glad greetings, Brit and Carlos poured out everything that had happened after the Millses had left Virginia City.

"If I'd known you two would get in such a peck of trouble, I never would have left," Mrs. Betsy said. "That poor child, losing her pa, then coming all this way and feeling she had to run away. What did you do to her?" She fixed an accusing gaze on Brit.

"I was such a dolt I didn't realize I loved her," Brit told them quietly. His feeling lit lamps behind his blue eyes.

"And what about this Dolores woman, Carlos's sister?" A glance at that young man's mouth hanging open showed Brit's revelation was news to him.

Brit smiled a little. "She is affianced to a wealthy hacienda owner. We have both changed." He left it like that.

"The greatest news, a gift from Dios, is that we are certain Señorita Joyous is my own cousin!" Carlos blurted out.

Mrs. Betsy's eyes popped and a warm smile creased her face when he explained. "Then I suggest you find her and tell her. . .many things," she sternly told them.

"We're hoping you remember the name of the town in southern California that she came from. Perhaps she has gone to the farm." Brit sighed and rubbed his hand across his eyes. He hadn't slept well since they reached Monterey. "Except how she would get there, I'm not for knowing. No young woman of her description has left Monterey, as far as we can discover."

"Try looking for a boy," Mrs. Betsy advised shrewdly. "Angus raised her to be canny. 'Twould be just like Joy to disguise herself and slip away." She thought hard. "Hmmm, if I remember right, that farm's somewhere down near the San Bernardino Valley. I can't remember if she ever mentioned the name of the village."

The next day the search for Joyous-Jessica-McFarlane-Montoya began in earnest when Carlos and Brit bid the Millses goodbye and headed south.

thirteen

The object of the search and joint heir to the Montoya estate along with Carlos and Dolores, wearily rode the new Jenny south and east. She avoided towns and villages except when she had to replenish her food supplies. Sometimes when her body grew weary, her heart sad from the events in Monterey, Joyous felt it had all been a jumbled dream and that in a little time she would reach the farm and find Daddy Angus waiting.

Hill and valley, desert and rich farmland knew the steady *clip clop* of Jenny's feet. The new burro resembled so much the faithful Jenny that Joy had left behind in Virginia City that the lonely young woman often wrapped her arms around her new friend and cried. Yet she never felt truly alone. She knew the spirit of her Friend and Master went with her.

Little by little, the two wanderers successfully covered the long trek toward home. The closer they got, the more real the farm became to Joy. Jogging along or walking beside Jenny, she made plans. She had no desire to oust the neighbor who leased the property. If they would simply make her welcome in their home—her home, actually—she would work hard as she had always done.

Her few needs could be easily met. Not a sigh escaped her lips for the fortune she had given up. It had seemed the right thing for her to do—it still did.

Joy's decision to disguise herself as a peon boy proved valuable. No one paid her the slightest attention beyond waiting on her when she timidly approached a store. California had many peon boys riding dusty donkeys. One more left no impression.

The hundreds of miles between Monterey and Los Vista, the village whose name Mrs. Betsy had struggled to remember, also provided time for Joy to think deeply about things eternal. She began to see her homeward journey as a parallel to her whole life's journey. Happiness and sorrow, mountains to climb, and pleasant valleys to cross matched the experiences she had had and would continue to experience before she reached the home prepared for those who remained faithful.

Gradually, the steady movement forward, no matter how slow, cleared her mind and helped her to understand: the importance in this and life's journey lay not in what she encountered but the way in which she responded. Many times she looked north and west toward the faraway place where those she loved dwelled. She changed from feeling ashamed at having fallen in love with Brit, who loved Dolores, to a proud acceptance that because of it, she had become a better and more understanding person.

Not fifty miles from Los Vista, Joy's first real setback

came. Sure-footed Jenny slipped on a rain-softened hillside and injured her right foreleg. Skilled fingers cared for the little burro's lame leg with hot compresses made from part of Joy's shirt tail and they lost a few days along their journey while Jenny made the most of a well-earned rest. At last they were ready to move on but Joyous refused to hurry. What difference did a day or so make? No one knew they were coming.

"Somewhere down near the San Bernardino Valley," Mrs. Betsy had said when she failed to remember the village near the McFarlane farm.

Brit and Carlos grimly decided to find that village if it took until snowfall. Yet the valley held many tiny hamlets and villages! Day after disappointing day they crisscrossed the spreading area, always asking for a prospector named McFarlane and his daughter Joyous. Always liquid black eyes and negative headshaking accompanied the sympathy in the faces of those questioned. Carlos proved to be invaluable with his ability to talk with those whose language Brit neither spoke nor understood.

"Señorita Joyous must be at her home by now," Carlos said reassuringly. "She will be glad to see us when we ride in on our good Sol and Shamrock."

"And if she's not for being there, what then?" Brit's face had thinned in their search. Shadows of regret for not knowing his own heart and recognizing Dolores to be

vain and shallow darkened his eyes. That uninformed
heart now beat fast with every remembrance of the desert
girl he had watched grow into womanhood, although
according to the dates Señora Montoya gave, Joy had
unknowingly passed her eighteenth birthday less than six
months before.

A new thought plagued him. At eighteen, Jessica
Montoya was an heiress and would be sought after by the
true-hearted and fortune-seeking alike. Would she feel
a man ten years older was too old for her? The troublesome idea buzzed in his brain like a pesky mosquito. He
said nothing to Carlos, who, in his fluent conversation,
painted rosy pictures and bright futures for them all.

"Except Dolores." Carlos scowled until his black
brows met." "She will do what Papa says, marry the so
rich señor and be petted and spoiled for the rest of her
life." He sighed and real concern for his sister erased his
happy expression. "Ah, if only once she could know what
it is to love another until that one's happiness is important, not just your own!" He irrepressibly added, "My
Sadie will be waiting. I say gracias to Dios every day of
my life for her—and for you, Señor Brit."

His comrade didn't speak. He simply held out his hand
and friendship flowed between them in the strong clasp.

Before leaving Monterey, Brit and Carlos had mapped
out their route so that if necessary, the Montoyas could

send messages to certain points to be picked up when the riders arrived. The two men faithfully checked but not until they reached San Bernardino itself did they find word from home. It contained good news and shocking news. Betsy Mills had finally remembered the name of Joy's village: Los Vista, just a few hours ride from San Bernardino!

The rest of the message read: *Find Jessica and return with her immediately. Ramon is very ill.*

"It is what we always feared," Carlos said. "All these years grieving for his lost *muchacha* has made him frail and weak. That is why Señora Mary looks so sad. Come!" He crammed his wide hat more firmly onto his head. "We must hurry."

Brit rode with a silent prayer on his lips, a prayer he couldn't have put into words but knew God heard. A dozen petitions blended and shifted into varying patterns, for Joy and the Montoyas, for himself and Carlos, who showed a deeper interest in hearing more of Jesus Christ than ever, for Sadie and Dolores and the Millses. Yet the seriousness of the news from Monterey couldn't control his unruly heart. It persisted in bouncing like a tumbleweed and became worse and worse the closer they got to Los Vista.

It took no time at all to find out from the storekeeper the location of the McFarlane farm. The friendly man was inclined to gossip, recalling all the years the prospector and Joy had lived there, then been gone. Brit and

Carlos finally managed to get away. By mutual unspoken agreement, once headed in the right direction they goaded Sol and Shamrock into a run that ate up the distance to the farm.

Well-tended fields and a trim low house attested to the stewardship of those who had cared for the place during the McFarlanes' absence. A round-faced Mexican and his ample-waisted wife came to the door in answer to the seekers' knock. Two *muchachos* peeped from behind their mother's skirts.

"We wish to see Señorita Joyous McFarlane," Carlos announced while Brit furiously tried to control his breathing.

"Señorita Joyous is not here. All these many years she and Señor Angus look for gold and silver," the surprised man told them in good English.

"Si. We hear they find much ore," his wife added.

Brit felt like Shamrock had unexpectedly given him a swift kick in the stomach. "She left Monterey many days ago," he said hoarsely. "She must be here!" Disappointment made way for worry. Even traveling slowly, Joy had been ahead of them a good week plus all the time they had wasted looking in the other parts of the valley.

The man looked sympathetic and opened wide the door. "Come in, come in. Señors will remain with us until she comes, si?"

For three days Brit and Carlos tarried, endlessly discussing what to do next. Carlos didn't want to leave. He felt sure Joyous would come soon. Brit frankly didn't know what to do. Perhaps the woman he loved never intended to return to the farm. Surely she wouldn't have set out for Virginia City, with winter lurking in the Sierra Nevadas! *God,* he prayed again and again, *forgive my blindness and help me find her.*

Those three days deepened his love. He remembered how his father had advised him to find a wife like his mother. He had been so dazzled by Dolores Montoya's beauty, he had run ahead of common sense. Now, every hour brought punishment. So did the urgent messages that continued to come from Monterey.

Carlos sent one back: *Tell Ramon. It might help.* The decision to do this had come after soul searching and the realization his uncle and aunt could suffer even more should they be unable to produce Joyous—and soon.

"If she doesn't come by tomorrow, I am going back," Brit grimly said one star-studded evening. He looked at the North Star.

"And then what?" Carlos demanded with the new forcefulness he had developed in the grueling search. "We know she did not go by stage or hired carriage."

Brit had no answer. He fell asleep only after putting Joyous in their Father's hands and admitting himself helpless to do more.

Worn out from his broken sleep and nightmares, Brit awakened late. The children had eaten breakfast and played outside the door. Their childish voices floated in his open window. Suddenly one piped in shrill treble, "Papa! Mama! *Burrito* come."

Burrito. Burro. Brit leaped from bed, hastily donned shirt and pants, stuffed sockless feet into his boots, and ran through the cool living room and out the door, heart pumping healthy red blood throughout his system and bringing him alive. He paused on the small porch. His spirits fell to the depths. Only a peon boy on a shaggy donkey, one of dozens he and Carlos had seen. Yet. . .he strained his eyes. Surely, the peon's clothing seemed familiar. The heavy jacket, the battered hat—hadn't Angus McFarlane worn them even after he possessed enough money to buy anything he wanted? Brit and Carlos used to tease the Scotsman who merely smiled and kept his own counsel.

"Joy?" His clear call straightened the drooping figure on the burro's back. The reins slipped through weak fingers. The rider swayed from obvious fatigue.

"Joy!" Brit leaped from the porch, ran to the girl whose blue eyes held shock. "*Mavourneen,* darling, we've been so worried." He caught her as she slid from Jenny.

"No." She thrust him away, horror filling her eyes and sponging away the radiant look he had seen for a moment. "You forget yourself and Dolores." She strumbled backwards until she pressed against Jenny's side.

Brit dropped his arms to his sides. His voice rang. "Dolores is affianced to a wealthy hacienda owner. I'm free."

The quiet words brought a flood of color to her dusty face. "But. . .you love her! You always have." She warded him off with both hands, the sturdy hands he loved.

He caught them close. "She dazzled me, like a falling star. Not until I returned did I see her as she is and realize the colleen who captured my heart had slipped away in the night." He placed his hands on her shoulders and gazed into her upturned face. "God is good, even to a thickheaded Irishman who has to be hit on the head before he knows what's best for him."

"Señorita Joyous!" Carlos bounded out of the house and over to them. "Are you not glad? You are my cousin, daughter of Uncle Ramon and his Señora, Mary." He spun her away from Brit, ignoring her protests. "The lace, it told the story."

He talked so rapidly Joy shook her head and Brit ordered, "Wait, Carlos. Let her be for getting her breath." He gently took her arm and led her to the house.

It took a full hour to make the tired traveler understand everything that had happened and to accept that she was Jessica Montoya. But her happiness died when she learned her real father lay ill in Monterey. She sprang to her feet, eyes flashing. "We must go, now."

"Si." Carlos nodded and talked with their host and hostess.

"If we hasten we can catch the stagecoach not far from here." He looked doubtful. "What of Sol and Shamrock?

They are tired and need rest."

"Leave them here," the round-faced Mexican suggested. "We will care for them and let them roll in rich grass until you return."

Before he finished speaking, Brit handed him far more money than such a service required, ignored his protests, and urged Joy to eat the quickly prepared but delicious meal set before them.

They caught the stagecoach with only minutes to spare and all the way north and west, discussed the bizarre turns of fate that led the three of them together by such strange paths.

"It is not fate but God," Joyous declared.

"Si." Now that the excitement had died down, Carlos tactfully pulled his sombrero low over his eyes, slumped in the seat opposite Brit and Joyous, and either slept or gave an excellent imitation of snoring.

Brit turned to her and said in a voice low enough not to reach the wily Carlos, should he be playing possum, "Could you ever be for caring about a man who loves you with all his heart but bears the weight of ten extra years?"

Her lips trembled. Her eyes looked like twin stars. "Mister O'Donnell, I'll be for confessing," she mimicked in his Irish brogue. "Daddy Angus and I prayed for someone to come and God sent you." A flush of color made her gilt freckles more pronounced than ever on her straight nose. "I hadn't bargained on it being a man who would one day be my. . .my husband," she faltered.

A quick glance at Carlos showed him relaxed and sprawled across the opposite seat. Again, money had ensured privacy. Brit cupped Joy's chin with one hand and lowered his face until his lips touched hers.

A snore broke off in the middle and changed to a delighted laugh. Then Carlos winked at the red-faced pair. "Ah, if only my Sadie could be here! 'Tis a grrr-and day it is, forrr the Irrrrish."

Even Brit's irritation with Carlos's hopelessly high spirits couldn't withstand the young man's terrible Irish accent. He placed an arm around Joy, drew her closer, and ordered, "Go back to sleep, you *spalpeen*."

"What's a *spalpeen*?" Carlos demanded, then grinned when Brit told him it meant an Irish rascal, in this case a Spanish rascal named Montoya.

Yet love and teasing couldn't overshadow the fear of what awaited them in Monterey. Joy's heart ached. Was she to learn her parents' identity then lose her father so soon? What would it be like to become Jessica Montoya again? A sob rose to her throat. No matter how much she came to love her real family, no one could ever replace Daddy Angus. Still, he would be happy that at last God had restored her to her family. She also knew that before long she would be neither McFarlane nor Montoya, but Mrs. O'Donnell—and she had a feeling he would never call her anything but Joyous. It comforted her, even when they reached Carlos's home and discovered that Ramon had briefly roused at the news Jessica had been found, only to pluck at his fine linen sheets and cry continuously for his lost child.

Don Carlos took one precious moment to fulfill his vow before hurrying them into a closed carriage to rush through the night to his brother's hacienda. "Can you ever forgive me?" he cried. His face twisted. "I did not know."

Joy had been prepared for this moment by Carlos, who frankly told her the whole story and added it was because of Dolores's jealousy that his papa had been swayed against her, along with his mama.

"There is nothing to forgive," she told the distraught, penitent man. "Please, take me to my father and mother." She barely noticed Dolores, who held back, or Inez, who had flown to her, entreating her forgiveness.

A swift journey delivered them to a hacienda whose door stood wide open in spite of the night's chill. Mary Montoya had put aside her mourning and stood in the warm, yellow glow of a fan light, wrapped in a white shawl, holding a torn, lace-trimmed dress. "Jessica." She held out her arms. "My daughter." The next instant Joyous stood wrapped in a mother's love for the first time in a long time, unable to do anything except cling to the tenderness even Brit's love for her could not surpass.

"We must go to Ramon," her mother whispered. She led the little party up a grand staircase whose fading splendor could be restored through the good fortune of the others and into an enormous bedroom dominated by a richly canopied bed.

The man in its depths looked more dead than alive except for his burning black eyes turned toward the doorway.

Joy saw the years of agony since she had been stolen engraved forever on Ramon's face. "Father?" She walked to the bed and knelt.

"Jessica." Life returned to the waxen face. A man who must be a doctor grunted approval. "Is it you?" Healing flamed in his countenance.

She threw back the old gray veil she still wore to keep out cold and too bold glances. Her glorious hair shimmered in the light of the hundred candles. "Father, I have come home."

From his vantage point near the door, Brit heard the sound of soft weeping. A verse from the Thirtieth Psalm that his mother had quoted many times in the hard years swept into his mind and blinded his eyes with mist not unlike that of Irish dells. *Weeping may endure for a night, but joy cometh in the morning.*

Joy had come to them all, a gift of God in the form of one in the morning of her life.

The veils that had hidden the past were cast aside, as one day earthly veils would be, leaving them face to face with the Heavenly Father who awaited their homecoming.

A Letter To Our Readers

Dear Reader:

In order that we might better contribute to your reading enjoyment, we would appreciate your taking a few minutes to respond to the following questions. When completed, please return to the following:

Karen Carroll, Editor
Heartsong Presents
P.O. Box 719
Uhrichsville, Ohio 44683

1. Did you enjoy reading *Veiled Joy*?
   ☐ Very much. I would like to see more books
   by this author!
   ☐ Moderately
   I would have enjoyed it more if _____

   _____

2. Are you a member of *Heartsong Presents*? Yes   No
   If no, where did you purchase this book? _____

   _____

3. What influenced your decision to purchase
   this book? (Circle those that apply.)

   Cover   Back cover copy

   Title   Friends

   Publicity   Other _____

4. On a scale from 1 (poor) to 10 (superior), please rate the following elements.

    ___Heroine   ___Plot

    ___Hero   ___Inspirational theme

    ___Setting   ___Secondary characters

5. What settings would you like to see covered in *Heartsong Presents* books?

    _____

    _____

6. What are some inspirational themes you would like to see treated in future books?_____

    _____

    _____

7. Would you be interested in reading other *Heartsong Presents* titles?   Yes   No

8. Please circle your age range:

Under 18	18-24	25-34
35-45	46-55	Over 55

9. How many hours per week do you read? _____

Name _____

Occupation _____

Address _____

City _____ State _____ Zip _____

add a little MYSTERY to your romance!

TWO GREAT INSPIRATIONAL ROMANCES WITH JUST A TOUCH OF MYSTERY
BY MARLENE J. CHASE

_____*The Other Side of Silence*—Anna Durham finds a purpose for living in the eyes of a needy child and a reason to love in the eyes of a lonely physician...but first the silence of secrets must be broken. HP6 BHSB-07 $2.95.

_____*This Trembling Cup*— A respite on a plush Wisconsin resort may just be the thing for Angie Carlson's burn-out—or just the beginning of a devious plot unraveling and the promise of love. HP5 BHSB-05 $2.95.

Inspirational Romance at its Best from one of America's Favorite Authors!

FOUR HISTORICAL ROMANCES
BY COLLEEN L. REECE

___ *A Torch for Trinity*—When Trinity Mason sacrifices her teaching ambitions for a one-room school, her life—and Will Thatcher's—will never be the same. HP1 BHSB-01 $2.95

__*Candleshine*-A sequel to *A Torch for Trinity*—With the onslaught of World War II, Candleshine Thatcher dedicates her life to nursing, and then her heart to a brave Marine lieutenant. HP7 BHSB-06 $2.95

__*Wildflower Harvest*—Ivy Ann and Laurel were often mistaken for each other...was it too late to tell one man the truth? HP2 BHSB-02 $2.95

____ *Desert Rose*-A sequel to *Wildflower Harvest*—When Rose Birchfield falls in love with one of Michael's letters, and then with a cowboy named Mike, no one is more confused than Rose herself. HP8 BHSB-08 $2.95